PRIME
TARGET

A CHASE

BY
DAN SCHMIDT

Prime Target
copyright © 2011 by Dan Schmidt

ISBN-13: 978-1466494817
ISBN-10: 1466494816

Cover image © Can Stock Photo Inc. / galdzer

WWW.TOUCANIC.NET

PRIME TARGET

A CHASE

Prologue

Nine Years Ago

Max squeezed the clutch lever, thumbed the kill switch and let his dirt bike coast to a stop. He put one booted foot on the ground and swung the other over the tail light, bringing it down in a single smooth motion on the kickstand. After checking to make sure the 350 would stay upright on the gravel shoulder, Max pulled off his helmet and hung it on a side mirror. He tugged at the zipper of his leather jacket and stared into the bush, keeping one ear cocked. Moments later, the thumping of another motorcycle drew closer. That would be Orange.

Other traffic wasn't likely on this remote side street at the edge of Carroll County; this neighborhood had been abandoned long ago. A developer had sailed in with a boatload of promises, but shortly after the roads went in, he and his earth-movers evaporated. Queries and investigations came up as empty as the bank accounts that funded those pre-construction down payments.

A different crowd moved in, guys Max knew. They used the web of pavement for short-track racing, demolition derbies and all manner of other foolishness, like the dark scrawl of names burned into the tarmac in front of him. Magnesium lifted from the high school physics lab: Unspool it on the ground to spell something, light one end and it burns so bright you can't watch. Brands the very surface on which others walk; makes you immortal. It also left a confession, which is why Max's name did not appear among those marking the street.

Orange pulled up and parked his bike

"Through here," Max said as his companion slid off his motorcycle. With a linebacker's build and the stealth of Cooper's Hawkeye, Orange followed as Max pushed through a curtain of vines and saplings.

Fifteen yards off the road, a tall, broad pine had bettered a car. The latter's hood had shaped itself to the former's girth and lost whatever comeliness it had been given at the factory. Each window was shattered, mushrooms grew in the upholstery. The body was pocked and rusty.

"Target practice," Max said, pointing at a scatter of rocks circling the vehicle.

Orange nodded sagely. "Close range."

"See if the VIN's still there, willya?" Max said, circling to the back of the crippled sedan.

The larger boy leaned over the hood to reach through what had once been the windshield. He brushed shards of safety glass off the cracked dash to uncover the thin metal strip with the vehicle's ID number. They would need that to collect the reward for finding a car presumed lost.

Max propped the sprung trunk lid open with a dead branch. He ignored the lures and hooks from an overturned tackle box, focusing instead on the slashed spare tire. Using a rock to loosen the wing nut holding it in place, Max he levered the wheel out of its well and reached down for a slim case that had been tucked beneath its concave rim.

Max grinned. He liked finding things.

-1

Present Day

A disheveled figure filled to overflowing a stool at one of the ubiquitous airport cafés, perfectly still in a concourse teeming with passengers, crew and employees.

He huddled over a tall paper cup. Its steam fogged the lenses of mirrored sunglasses pinned to his head by a khaki hat with fuzzy ear flaps which covered only part of the Einstein hair. A herringbone overcoat stained by an oil slick between the shoulder blades wrapped him like a blanket and Army fatigues tucked into unclasped rubber boots. Either he hadn't noticed the warming weather outside, or he simply lacked a choice of clothing. The man sat alone, assured of a wide berth from other customers repelled by his clothing and offended by his smell.

Commotion in the bright hall stirred the man from his meditation. Lime-shirted Japanese tourists waving orange flags formed a citrus tidal wave rolling in his direction. An incandescent redhead led them. With one hand she clutched the strap of a bulging shoulder bag, with the other she held aloft a larger version of the triangular flag. Imposing as a locomotive's cowcatcher, the woman cleared a path for the mob that followed.

Her long stride had the Asians jogging. She barked commands which ricocheted off the ceiling and slammed into her followers, urging them to keep up, keep moving so that they could all make their gate on time. The redhead's voice cut through hallway clatter like a concrete saw.

Little more than air passed through this crowd as eager tourists sprawled across the corridor's width, slowing traffic to a crawl in both directions. Only a few on their way to a gate or the baggage area managed to find fissures in the mass and dart through. A traveler, blond and much taller than the Asians, strode up from behind, anxiously seeking such a gap. He looked like a college student, given the frayed sweater, jeans and sandals; he held a polished briefcase against his chest. One of the green shirts near the corridor's wall stumbled, and companions around her paused for a moment. Seizing the opportunity, the student sped toward the narrow opening.

Further down the concourse, the vagabond rose from his stool. Dragging his enormous cup off the counter, he stepped into the hallway, directly into the oncoming student's path. The impact of their collision was audible. Coffee exploded, showering several nearby Japanese whose shrieks stopped the tour guide so abruptly that those behind her toppled the redhead to the floor. More shrieking followed as bodies piled up.

The pungent, shabby man disappeared with the student beneath a tangle of limbs. People nearby got sucked into the writhing mass while those at its outer edge whipped out cameras. Excitement intensified when the mob realized their tour guide had fainted.

An airport security guard twenty gates away had watched the surge of humanity moving toward him; when it stopped, he decided to investigate. He waded into the confusion, his walkie-talkie belching static. A pair of golf carts with flashing yellow lights rolled up in his wake.

The circle of gawkers around those who had fallen was expanding, so the guard wasn't sure where to start his effort to restore order. He noticed a young man, very tall, trying to penetrate the crowd. His eyes swept the floor, searching. A contact lens maybe, or a dropped magazine?

"My briefcase." The guard's uniform made this traveler nervous; he wiped his palms on his jeans as he spoke to the official, shuffled his sandaled feet, pulled at the cuffs of his shirt. "I cannot locate it." The voice had an accent the guard could not place.

"They's no need to worry, son. We'll find it." He hiked his striped pants up by a wide black belt and sniffed. "Jes' what exactly it look like?"

"Yes, well," the foreigner began. Then he coughed into the sleeve of his sweater, rubbed his forehead and adjusted a pair of wide-armed glasses. "That odd fellow who hit me, he is one of your homeless people, perhaps? Where has he gone?"

The portly man's brow wrinkled. "Homeless guy in here? No idea. Hang on a sec." The knot of people gathered around the prone tour guide was loosening, so the guard managed to weave through them and pop out at the far side, near the parked golf carts.

"Any of you seen some other guy crawling around?" he asked the suits. He jerked a thumb over his shoulder. "Kid says he's lost a briefcase, too."

One of the officials barked, "Impossible to find anything in this mess til you clear things up."

Another was tapping furiously on his phone's keypad. A third motioned to the flame-haired woman who was rising unsteadily to her feet. "Have you checked on her yet?"

The security guard turned back to the crowd. His hat and badge allowed him to worm through the tightly packed tourists. Reaching the woman in a few strides, he offered a hand as she rose. "There now, let's take it easy, ma'am."

She smiled, clutching the guard's beefy arm.

He patted her hand. "Any chance you seen some homeless guy get knocked down in all this?"

The woman's blank stare was not unexpected. As the guard was repeating his question, a high-pitched squeal pierced the air, bringing a sudden hush in the corridor. Then the vacuum filled with excited babble. Turning toward the wall of sound, the guard followed a score of pointing fingers. He motioned for the tour guide to stay where she was, then knifed his way through more bodies to investigate. As the officials in the golf cart craned their necks for a look, the angular blond who had lost a briefcase began to sidle away from the crowd.

At the far wall, leaning against a pillar, a young executive was murmuring into his cell, bemused by the turmoil. A bright splatter tie punctuated his dark suit and shirt; his short brown hair had been styled by a hurricane.

Watching the crowd with mild interest, this traveler had noticed the student's futile search. He saw the young man pause from his labors, pat his back pocket and realize something else was missing. The blond tried again to penetrate the knot of babbling people, but failed. With this new excitement, the ranks in front of him had closed even tighter. He actually jumped, in an effort to better assess the situation, but there was no breaking through. Shaking his head, radiating despair, he pivoted and set off instead toward the baggage claim area.

The guard, alerted by pointing tourists, had discovered a mound of clothes. He poked at it with his foot, probing for a body. Nearby, a tourist bent to retrieve a khaki hat behind a trash can. She pulled at the thick wig sewn to its ear flaps, turning it over for better leverage. That dislodged sunglasses which fell to the floor. Mirrored lenses shattered. Startled, the guard stepped back from the pile of clothing. There was no strange body, homeless or otherwise. No sign of a briefcase, either.

Finished with his call, the wind-blown executive snapped shut his cell phone and slipped it into his coat pocket. He grabbed the handle of a bulky travel bag and kicked its base to angle away from him. Smirking at the confusion, he headed for the terminal's exit.

A few yards away, the tour guide had fully recovered. At her command, every lime T-shirted tourist collected bags set down during the show. Those with flags raised and waved them. Fingers went to the redhead's mouth for an ear-splitting whistle, and then she set off down the concourse with the determination of an Army cadet. The guard, unsure who to detain, scratched the stubble at his chin.

Splatter-tie looked back briefly and caught the redhead's eye. Her face did not change, but on his, a faint smile formed. At this distance, in this light, he had to admit that she really did look quite beautiful.

"I can't believe you pulled that off. In public, with so many people around."

"More's the better, I always say, and you know I love an audience. Besides, I had some help."

"True that. But still."

A dark suit jacket hung on the back of a folding metal chair, draped by a brightly splotched tie. Standing on the opposite side of the kitchen table, a young man wearing latex gloves thumbed through a battered wallet. Cuffs rolled, his white shirt was open at the collar. He tossed the billfold into a shoe box, then pulled a black briefcase closer and squared it before him on the table. Its shiny latches remained shut. Bending over the case, the young man used the knife selected from his multi-tool to cut a large U. He peeled back a film of pebbled vinyl and pinned it to the table with the shoebox.

"I never did get why people bother with locks for these things," he said.

Backlit in the doorway, a woman shook her head, combing fingers through pepperoni hair.

"Maybe they plan to use them again?"

"Hmph." The blade probed deeper. Strong fingers slid into the slit to pry up an edge. With three deft cuts he freed a square of cardboard and flipped it toward the sink behind him. From inside he pulled out a pair of Italian novels, a notepad, file folders, a bag of nuts and raisins, a calculator, and a zippered pouch. He tipped the case and felt one more object slide toward him. A cigar box.

"Dutch Masters," he said, breaking the seal. "Nice touch."

2

Pieter de Groot spat blood to the cement floor. "I told you—"

A blow to the face interrupted his attempt to explain.

Pieter's head lolled. He found linear thought difficult. How had this happened? A graduate assistant in history, he specialized in astronomy during the Enlightenment. That interest had taken him to Italy, for research on the link between his famous countryman Christiaan Huygens and the Italian Giovanni Cassini, both of whom had been intrigued by Saturn.

But now Pieter, strapped to a chair, was being pummeled by a man with bricks for hands. His speech came out thick. "If you keep hit—"

Another vicious strike. De Groot felt his jaw loosening. A week ago he had been in Venice, at a pub with pulsing music, flowing beer, and pretty waitresses, unwinding after several months of intense study. Soon he would be back at his university in The Hague, but new friends he'd made in Italy had taken him to the pub to meet a man who seemed at the time to be quite charming. He had asked many questions about Pieter's studies, about his aspirations, about his family.

Pieter had been especially proud to mention that he had relatives in the United States.

Toward the end of the evening, the man had made an unusual offer: would Pieter be interested in a free trip to America? All he need do was to carry a package on the plane. The man making the offer explained that transporting the package was urgent but that he was unable to travel. Pieter could take his place, using a ticket that would permit flight as far as Los Angeles. Of course, there would first be a stop in Baltimore, but hadn't Pieter spoken of relatives in a town near there? He would deliver the package then, after which he could continue his journey. A pleasant arrangement, was it not?

The offer had sounded splendid; Pieter yearned for a diversion before returning to the dull routine of lecturing first-year students. He had also watched too many spy movies not to be a little intrigued, and his sense for adventure had trumped common sense. He agreed to the terms immediately, assuring himself that he was only an ordinary university student. What possible harm could come of this?

Another question disrupted his recollections and brought him back to the present. In this windowless space, without his glasses, hit repeatedly by a pile driver, his vision blurred, his head throbbed.

"You have the key. Did you open the case?"

"I have the key so that I could comply with customs officials, but they did not ask. Nor did I see what was inside."

"Did you give the case to someone else? Did you sell it for more money?"

Pieter tried to focus on his questioner; one eye had swollen shut, tears streamed from the other. Blood was pooling in his mouth again.

"No, as I told you before, I—"

A movement to one side caught his attention; he flinched. The broad hand connected again.

Stars, Pieter de Groot thought as consciousness slipped away. How ironic for one fascinated by the night sky. You really do see stars.

The student's questioner sighed. "Rather overmuch, I'm afraid. Still, I'm not sure he has any information of value. Once again, Trevor, we seem to be falling short."

The soft voice was tinged with sadness and nearly swallowed by the cavernous room. It came from a slight man standing in the shadow of his enormous companion. He looked at the slumped figure of de Groot, and then let his gaze roam. Except for a dump truck, a pair of fifty-gallon drums, and a light blue minivan, the three of them were alone in this abandoned repair shop.

"A most tiresome place." The words came out with effort. Long fingers smoothed the fringe of hair that touched his shirt collar. He was overdue for a proper barber. "I suppose he's dead?"

His companion stepped closer to the body in the chair. "I don't believe so. I only—"

"I know, Trevor, I know. Infrequent blows to the head, as we agreed. However, the force of this last application was rather excessive. Perhaps you do not know your own strength?"

"It's not strength, Mr. Cumin. It's location. The fellow jerked a bit there that last time, and while I attempted to recalibrate, his twitching meant I inadvertently struck the forehead. It's his own fault, really. Had he stayed still, the impact would have fallen only on his cheek. Nevertheless, I should think he's merely stunned." Trevor placed two fingers on de Groot's carotid artery and nodded. "As I surmised."

"Very well." Mr. Cumin adjusted the scarf tucked beneath his charcoal overcoat. This entire country chilled him. "We must be on our way." The dismal surroundings amplified his morose mood. His head drooped, and he noticed a smudge on the toe of his wingtip. Cumin put a hand on de Groot's inert shoulder to steady himself, raised the foot, and wiped it on the trousers of the man tied to the wooden chair. "We'll have to request copies. I don't imagine she'll be pleased by that."

Trevor retrieved a cap resting on one of the oil drums and headed toward the blue minivan. He stepped into the vehicle and started the motor. His companion entered after brushing the seat.

"Have you taken in a cat, Trevor?"

The other man frowned. "Now what would I do with a pet, Mr. Cumin?"

Only one person in the alley noticed the minivan pull out of the warehouse. He also had blurred vision, but for a different reason. The thimbleful of alcohol-free molecules in his brain registered surprise that a vehicle was leaving Mike's place. Cars don't, he thought. Cars won't. Good mechanic, that Mick. Mike. If I had a car, I'd. It's late. My head.

The man backed to a brick wall and slid to the ground. A hand slipped into the torn pocket of his coat, fished through crumpled paper to pat smooth glass. Good. Still there.

A phone purred. The tray holding it had been carved from cocobolo removed from a Central American rain forest by entrepreneurs who harvested on behalf of wealthy patrons. Cocobolo's streaks of color—yellow, gray, dark brown, purple—were unusual for wood and of great interest to people like the Belgian financier working in South America who originally commissioned this piece. A craftsman had shaped and sanded until the wood was smooth as soapstone and thin as paper. The imposing granite slab of the desk where the tray now sat provided a pleasing contrast.

The woman who reached for the phone took care not to mar the tray's shine with fingerprints. She admired this sculpture in wood; cocobolo's uniqueness suited her, soothed her.

"We have the second courier, but not his case."

"Experiencing difficulties?" The woman at the granite desk felt her pulse quicken. She did not care for problems.

"More of a challenge."

"Indeed."

"Apparently he was the victim of a random pickpocket, or another party is attuned to our interests."

"Both are irrelevant."

"Shall I stay the course?"

"The question need not be posed."

"Very well. I'm sorry to put you out, but we find ourselves in need of another set."

She paused, disturbed by the irregularity. Was there no end to this bumbler's ineptitude? Her eyes flitted to the delicate sandpiper perched on a nearby bookshelf. She closed her mouth and breathed deeply through her nose, starting the rhythm her Hatha yoga instructor had taught.

The sandpiper had been sculpted from a hawksbill turtle's shell, long after the international ban on items derived from tortoise shell had been enacted. She admired the fine workmanship, and marveled again at the paradox of using a sea creature to fashion a shore bird. Her heart rate slowed, balance returned.

"I shall have the Frenchman call with details. But I would not expect this to happen again." She slid the phone shut and returned it to the cocobolo tray. Afternoon light made the variegated wood shimmer. Raise arms over head slowly; stop when palms meet. Inhale deeply, through the nose. Hold. Exhale. She particularly admired the band of crimson.

Corporal Fire Davis switched off the squad car's engine. He really liked these new hopped-up vehicles. Thick-muscled fenders with a front grill solid as redwoods said, 'we're all business, baby.' Matte black finish made the rig easy to hide in shadows, but there was also a full spectrum of lights and half a thousand horses when he had to break cover.

On the long afternoons Fire sat behind the billboard at the edge of town, he imagined his foot to the floor, the car's predatory hood out in front of the siren's scream, tach pegged, in pursuit. Zero to awesome in under six seconds, his mind as focused as a laser. He held the leather-wrapped wheel in a rock-steady grip. Roma, who would be sitting next to him for some as-yet-unaccountable reason, would admire the skill.

"Hey, partner. You going inside, or what?"

Archibald Davis interrupted Fire's reverie. The two rode together, much to the latter's dismay. They shared a last name, too, but this pair of officers on Glenford's police force was not related. While this gave Fire no end of relief, it also confused people in and around the department, so Fire took every opportunity to set the record straight. Anyone could see there was no resemblance, he would say to those who even began to ask the question. I work out, I'm young, have all my hair. Archie lives on tacos and Twinkies, so when it comes to body mass index? And two stripes, Fire would say, pointing to his shoulder. In one year. Archie's just counting the days til he can turn in his badge and watch cable from his recliner. No, we are not related. It's just that Davis is a really common name. OK?

Fire had taken the job after finishing community college; it would be a stepping stone to the Academy in New York or Texas, and from there, who knew? Granted, pulling duty with a pastry junkie minutes away from retirement was a far cry from the mentor he'd imagined, but things would work out. Fire would endure Archibald Davis, and others would recognize his patience in the face of this adversity. But every once in a while, Fire thought as he pulled the key out of the ignition, it would be nice for Arch to haul his fat self out of the car soon enough to back him up.

"Got it."

Fire cracked the door with one hand, retrieved his cap from the dash with the other. Its dark green fabric, illumined by a gold GPD logo stitched above the bill, made him feel ominous. Roma liked this cap. At least, he was pretty sure she did.

The building was familiar. Mike had taken him in after high school, given him a job while Fire studied and worked out in preparation for his life's calling. Good mechanic, lousy business sense that Mike. Fire knew some online courses that might have benefited him, but no, Mike weren't going to no school. Better to close the place than fight the suits, Mike had said, more than once. He sure showed them.

Now Mike's Garage was a vacant shell where kids hung out on weekends and homeless people flopped until somebody got a nose out of joint. Mike sold plumbing fixtures on the Eastern shore almost an hour's drive one way. A long commute, especially in winter. Misplaced pride, Fire thought. Better to have some ambition and pursue your dreams. That made him think of Glenford which, he knew, was pretty much a one-horse town. He'd stay to learn all he could, and then move up and out. Meanwhile, having Roma nearby helped.

The radio had crackled earlier, breaking the morning's boredom during the routine trolling of the downtown shopping district. This was their regular beat, courtesy of Glenford's mayor who used cops to keep merchants happy and tourists coming back. Everybody felt better with a hulking police cruiser doing laps.

"Davis, Davis." Myra, the dispatcher, could not get enough of this pair. "Had a call about Mike's Garage. Some guy says he heard gunshots 'bout fifteen minutes ago. Get yoursefs down there pronto." Myra had no schooling in proper radio protocol.

"10-4." Fire hit the turn signal. He couldn't floor the squad in town, but he'd get close. Archibald knew what was coming.

"Hold on, pard," he pleaded. He wrapped the Boston cream from his second breakfast in a fresh napkin and set it on the dash, then ratcheted the special-order cup holder tighter around the Styrofoam full of his java. They were on Market's four-lane. Arch took the shoulder belt in his fleshy right hand and with his left pointed through the windshield. "Make it so."

Fire flipped the siren, punched the gas. They blew through the lights at Jefferson, Madison and Lincoln and nearly T-boned a blue minivan that tried to turn the corner ahead of them at Harrison.

"Can you believe that guy?" Archie yelled. "Like he can't see us." He swiveled to look as they sped past but the van was pure vanilla, occupied by a couple of startled carpoolers.

Fire, mute, calculated angles and velocity, his eyes darting right and left. Check the rearview, spot the tach, goose the throttle. At Washington, he stood on the brakes and smoked the tires with a right turn. Archie's donut slid out of the napkin and into the crack between vinyl and glass, wedged out of reach.

The siren went silent and Fire cut the lights. They had crawled down the block before easing into the alley, then stopped a few yards from Mike's. Now they sat outside the garage, ready to investigate. Arch invited Fire, once again, to be his guest.

Fire stepped out of the car. Hang on: did Myra say gunshots?

He backed up and slid into the cruiser. "Think I'll take this," he said, flipping the latches on the 12-gauge strapped to the console rack.

"Good plan," Archie said. He unclipped his seat belt and scooted forward to scrape chocolate off the windshield. Licking his fingers, smacking his lips, Archie muttered, "Right with you, pard." Then the round-bellied cop pulled at the door handle. "Ready?"

The pair approached the building's side entrance. Fire ducked under the door's window and flattened himself against the brick exterior. Archie turned the knob. "Locked," he said.

Fire lifted his chin to indicate the large bay a few yards down from the door his partner had tried. It stood wide open.

"Right behind you, Byron," Archibald whispered, a hand glued to his holster.

The younger man grimaced. He hated his given name, especially when used by this other Davis. *Fire* was a much better fit. More policial. Policial. It was a word Fire made up, but one he liked to use.

Sliding along the unpainted cinder block, Fire held the shotgun across his chest. When he came to the wide opening, he stopped, then ducked his head inside for a moment. "Looks empty," he said.

"You sure?" Archie asked.

"Feel free," Fire said. "Look for yourself."

"I trust you, pard." Arch's voice dropped. "Now what?"

Fire, silent, folded more of his body around the entrance. When it didn't get blasted, he poured the rest of himself into the dusty space. He saw a dump truck, squat barrels and a wooden chair tipped on its side. But no people, unless they were in the truck.

Dump truck?

"Hit the deck!" Fire commanded, pulling Archie to the floor and rolling toward a steel pillar that supported the roof. Not much cover.

Fire's partner went down hard. "My knee!" he howled.

"Quiet." Fire's whisper was fierce.

"Or what, you maniac? If there was somebody in that truck, they'd a picked us off like squirrels. Only thing we proved so far is that you can roll in dirt and my knee is softer than cement. Congratulations, Byron. Now you get to carry me back to the squad."

Fire stood, brushing grit from his khakis. The 12-gauge had clattered against the metal wall. He made a mental note: Next time, hold on to the gun. Checking that Archie hadn't noticed, he retrieved it and then went to make sure the dump truck was empty.

Satisfied, Fire walked over to the chair, ignoring the other man's theatrical moans. Patches of dirt bore faint footprints; probably kids goofing around. He bent to right the chair and noticed a stain on the floor.

"Is that—?" Archie had limped up behind him, dragging one foot across the concrete floor like Quasimodo. Fire pulled a plastic bag from his uniform's shirt pocket. Who said a beat cop couldn't aspire to detective work? He flipped open the blade from the Leatherman at his belt and scraped up a penny-sized sample.

"Blood for sure," Fire said, zipping the bag shut. "Fresh, too."

He backed away slowly from the chair without touching the wood and felt a lump under the heel of his left shoe. More evidence. Fire spun on his toe and gave the object a wide berth, then reached down. Using the Leatherman's pliers, he pinched a pair of glasses. Both of the wide arms were twisted, like they'd been stepped on.

"Someone's been here, Davis," Fire said. He only acknowledged his partner's last name at times of grave importance.

"That's some first-rate detecting, Sherlock." Archie said. "I'll call it in."

3

The driver's license of MacGregor McCheyne MacAllister blared with his ancestry, as did his passport, credit card statements and every other legal document that identified him to the appropriate banking or government agency. Since elementary school, the name had been a burden, and while it was briefly intriguing when he started college, he had grown tired of its ridiculous length and patent ethnicity. It was simply too much information, this eight furlong name that recalled both his paternal and maternal grandfather. Too many Macs. But eventually he'd discovered a way out of the dilemma; Max was good at finding things.

He lived in a storage barn on his parents' farmette. They'd moved out of the suburbs to reclaim this place that had long been in the family, and Max had asked for space after he'd had enough of college. His dad, the orthodontist, was reluctant to give up a room in the main house, saying that he liked an empty nest. Instead, he offered Max the old storage barn, which also housed the dormant tractor.

Unwilling to share his living quarters with farm implements, Max found a book on engine repair at the library. For good measure, he also tore the tractor's body apart and painted it blue, like the original. When it started on the first try, Max drove over to the working barn. His father, impressed, asked if he wanted to hook up the plow. Max shook his head.

"You're the farmer," he'd said, leaping down from the metal seat.

Then he set to work on the rest of the ramshackle place, raking out a decade's worth of animals, vegetables and minerals. He heavied up the electrical service, installed triple-paned windows, and cut a hole for the woodstove's flue. A buddy in town found a discarded satellite dish, so he bolted that to a pole and hacked free service. From a pile of lumber and plastic sheeting next to the shed, he salvaged enough material for a lean-to to protect his dirt bike and the Datsun.

Furniture he scavenged from dumpsters and curbsides. Thrift stores, too, where he picked up an oak dresser that had been painted pink. Stripped, polished with tung oil and fitted with shiny brass hardware, the piece sold online for enough to cover his costs and then some.

For more serious income, Max had his uncle.

"What's in the box?"

The flame-haired woman had followed Max to the back wall of the converted barn. His desk, an ancient wooden door perched on two sawhorses, was crowded with an assortment of models, books, magazines and electronics. Max laid the cigar box near the scanner and pulled out the desk chair. Its rusty spring creaked as he sat; he held its wooden armrests, filling his palms with their curves. Then he leaned forward and twiddled a mouse. The monitor's amber light changed to green.

"We'll know in a minute, but I'm thinking—" Max lifted the scanner's lid and then reached for the case. "Yep. Pictures."

"Pictures? That's it?"

"You were expecting diamonds? Rubies? The key to a bus depot locker or safe deposit box? A Maltese falcon, maybe?"

"Well," she said, pouting. "I figured what with asking Martina if I could sub for her at the airport and then having to change my hair, there would be.... Wait a minute. I got this tomato dye job just so you could swipe a few pictures?"

The chair groaned as he swiveled to face her. "Actually, that color was so you wouldn't get noticed."

Hands went to hips, her head tilted, and her mouth scrunched to one side in a 'You're kidding, right?' pose.

Max leaned back, to more squeaking. "Yeah, I know, who wouldn't notice the hair? But that's the point. The more outlandish, the more people only remember what's obvious, and what you can change. It's like this: ask the people in the scrum at the airport what they saw and most of them will say 'a lady with red hair.' Ask for more details, like eye color, height, distinguishing marks? All they noticed was the hair."

"Or splatter tie?"

"Or splatter tie." Max smiled, and returned to the scanner. "By the way," he said. "These pictures are more than snapshots. They're clues about where our guy is going next."

"Clues?" She chewed her lip. "Are you working for dear Mr. Bedford again?"

Max had paused at the last of the pictures from the box. His eyes narrowed, he began drumming the door that served as a desk, and all other sensory data went unnoticed. The woman cleared her throat.

"Earth to Max, earth to Max." She whistled loud enough to crack glass.

He jumped in his chair. "What?"

"I said, are you working for Uncle Sty?"

"Uh, yeah." He regained composure, reloaded the scanner and turned back to the computer. "You want to see it bigger?"

She had waited before, for her compulsively meticulous brother to examine this, or build that, or investigate some sort of incredibly fascinating, excruciatingly boring object or possibility. What kept him up nights put her to sleep in minutes. So no thanks, not today.

"I need to go." She shouldered her white bag and fished for the sunglasses tangled in her hair. "It'll take hours to get this color back to normal."

"I kinda like it," Max said over his shoulder.

"You like Naugahyde and avocado appliances, too, so I'm not trusting fashion advice from your corner. Call me when you know what's going on?"

"Sure."

The young woman retreated through the kitchen area, pausing to open the refrigerator. "You want me to bring over a casserole? You could stand some real food in this place."

He said nothing, peering instead at the monitor as a picture formed, a few lines at a time.

She shut the fridge and opened a cupboard door. Enough vegetable soup, ramen, and peanut butter to survive for a month. Yuk. At the door, she held the knob. "See you later?"

A picture filled the flat screen in front of Max, but she was too far away to make out details. He rose to lay another photo on the scanner bed and noticed her about to go.

"You're leaving?"

"Yes," she said, patient from practice. "Did you want to meet for supper this evening?"

"Can't," he said. "Gotta work."

"Suit yourself. How about later in the week?"

"Maybe."

She twisted the knob. "OK. See ya."

He mumbled, engrossed in other interests.

"Ciao," she said.

The door closed as he called out, "Bye, Roma." He took his seat again in front of the large glowing screen as a new picture began to take shape.

His sister phoned two days later, after Max had sent copies of the pictures to his uncle.

"How about a pizza at Rico's tonight?" she asked. By then he'd had a reply from his uncle that put things in motion.

"Can't," Max said. "I've got a plane to catch."

"What time is your flight?"

" 'Bout nine, out of BWI."

"Where to?" she asked.

"Michigan."

"What for?"

"Can't say, not until later."

Max could hear her pout. "Rico's is fast. Meet me at six, we can eat before you go."

Max arrived at Rico's late, left his well-used, dearly loved 280Z in the alley, and sprinted for the door. He spotted Roma instantly in the small place; the person in the booth with her made him grunt.

"Hey," he said to her, and then he nodded curtly to the fellow seated across from her. "Orange." Max looked back at his sister. "You didn't say—"

Roma put down the menu she had been studying. A pretense, since Max knew she only ordered vegetable pizzas. "It's time you got over this childish behavior," she told him.

"I'm up for that." The guy with Roma laid his forest green cap on the plastic bench seat and stuck out a hand. "What do you say, Max? Can't we be friends again?"

Before Max could reply, a voice mellowed by Chianti floated over from the counter behind him. "Hey Roma, honey, we got nice sausage, fresh this morning. You want I should put it on your pizza?"

Roma blinked, turned to face the man whose arms were floured up to his elbows. "No, Rico. You know I don't eat meat."

"How about you, officer? You want something you can sink your teeth into?"

The young man across from Max's sister shook his head, and Rico returned to twirling pizza dough on his balled fists.

Max still stood, his gaze shifting between the two people in the booth. "We've been over this," he said. "There's still that thing, that time."

"With that girl?" Orange asked.

"But that's old news," Roma protested. "Just because—"

"Just because Orange here made me look like an idiot?"

"Max." Orange's face matched close-cropped hair the color of a maple tree in fall. More pain than discomfort registered. "That was like five years ago, and I told you I was sorry."

"Yeah, well." Max's shoulders hunched.

Orange and Max had been friends as long as either could remember. After Orange's parents split up when he was ten, Orange stayed in town with his dad but mostly lived at Max's house. Whatever scheme Max cooked up, Orange was at his side, loyal and unflappable. Max wanted to build a tree house, Orange hauled lumber; Max planned a ride to Myrtle Beach over a long weekend, Orange took the test for a license and spent his accumulated allowance on a motorcycle; Max figured out there was a bounty on stolen cars, Orange watched his back and helped with paperwork.

They went in separate directions after high school, but their friendship disintegrated because of Orange. Or so Max saw it, after his former friend started dating the girl Max had intended to marry.

"You never asked her, Max," Roma said. "You only had one date."

"But he knew," Max whispered, slanting his head toward her companion.

Orange rubbed one palm against another, washing his hands without water or soap. He nodded. "Yeah. But I'd been walking in your shadow so long that I decided just once I'd move out in front. Like

Roma says, you never did declare yourself, so I asked her. Mostly to prove I didn't always have to follow you." His head fell to his chest. "We went out a couple times, but my heart wasn't in it. Nice girl, but my motives were crummy."

Max was staring at Orange. Usually this guy who in high school had been his friend and partner in mischief didn't talk so much.

"Whatever I won with that wasn't worth losing my best friend." Orange coughed. "Decided at that point I wouldn't ever get in your way again."

"That's why you stopped dating?" Max asked.

The man nodded, the muscles in his forearms tensing as he flexed and clenched his fingers. "And why the only girl I even thought about after that was totally safe." He glanced at Roma, who was staring at a salt shaker.

"Totally safe," Max said. "But completely out of reach." He pulled car keys from his pocket, spun on his heel and sped out the door.

Orange watched him go, his mouth open, eyes blinking.

Once the door thumped shut after Max's sudden departure, Roma turned back to Orange. "Not completely," she said.

4

The car ride, with both windows down and the stereo cranked, calmed him. By the time Max reached Baltimore Washington International airport, he was willing to concede that Orange really wasn't the jerk Max wanted him to be. In fact, he might actually have a point. Maybe Max had problems with commitment and just needed someone to blame. He'd ponder that further, as soon as he finished this job for Uncle Sty.

Max parked the Datsun in an overnight lot and caught a shuttle to the terminal. The lines were thin, so Max breezed through security. On the first leg of his flight, the adjacent seat was empty, which gave him space to arrange his thoughts.

Tonight at Rico's had been the longest conversation he'd had with Orange in five years. *Five years*? Max went back to that fateful week during his sophomore year in college, starting with his visit to the house Orange had bought that winter.

They had been standing in the kitchen when Orange explained his purchase of the modest Cape Cod not far from the community college. "First the cage, then the bird," he had murmured.

"What was that?" Max had asked.

Orange's freckles darkened. "I read it someplace."

Max chuckled. "Anyone in particular?"

His friend's head was down; he spoke to the linoleum. "Possibly." The word was barely audible, and Max steered the conversation to other topics. He liked the brick exterior and living room's stone hearth. The high ceilings were a bonus. He suggested that Orange tear up the ratty carpet and buff out the hardwood floors beneath it.

They'd parted friends, but Friday, while Max was at the mall shopping for clothes to take back to college, he'd seen Orange, standing with Zeta Charles in front of a store window. Holding her hand. Zeta Charles, who had been in Max's high school senior English class, and who had not escaped his notice.

He'd raced back to Orange's new house later that evening and pounded on the door, nearly bowling the larger boy over with his accusations.

"What are you doing?" Max had yelled. "You knew I had my eye on... on...." He reined in the hands that had been gesturing wildly, sticking them in the back pockets of his jeans. As Max remembered it, Orange had simply stared at him, silent. In all the years Max had known him, Orange had never lost his temper, never yelled, not even during football season.

Once Max had sputtered to a stop, Orange said, "Is this about Zeta?"

"Are you totally dense?" Max's hands were slicing the air, but he could think of nothing more to say.

Orange leaned against the door jamb. "I'm sorry, Max. If you want, I'll tell her you're planning to call."

Max's jaw dropped, but still he did not speak. Instead, he turned his back on Orange, stumbled down the front steps and drove away from a friendship that had started in kindergarten. Orange had phoned, tried to apologize again, but Max was adamant. He returned to college, made other friends, and when that phase ended, dove into work. Orange was history.

Living back at home, however, put him in the neighborhood, so Max saw Orange occasionally. More than once, he had spotted his former friend in the company of his sister, but had given that little consideration, until tonight. Max thought back on the way Orange had looked at Roma, and how she returned his gaze with more than a passing interest.

Wait a minute. As long as he and Orange had been friends, Roma was always the annoying baby sister. Max ignored her as inherently boring; he presumed Orange had done the same. *What if*—? Max slapped his head. For someone who was supposed to be good at finding things, he had missed this.

But Max wasn't prepared to follow that line of reasoning to its logical end. Later, he told himself, after this job is over. He pulled a magazine from the seat pocket and turned to the crossword, willing his mind to shift into a different gear. The plane soon landed in Cincinnati, and after a brief stop was on its way again. Shortly before midnight, Max was pulling out of the Grand Rapids airport in a rental.

With the car on cruise, Max checked for messages. Only one, quickly read. After tapping a reply, he concentrated on the road. In Holland, another hour west, there would be a cheap room for a few hours' sleep before the morning game.

The insurance company's branch office in western Montana was a long way from northern Virginia.

Stuyvesant Bedford still had days when he couldn't believe he lived here now. In a cabin with a view of Flathead Lake? Amazing. After years in airplanes, fleabag hotels, and trapped behind a desk underground, this place where you could stare out a window into forever caught him by surprise every time. It didn't take long to figure out why the license plates read 'Big Sky State'.

When you weren't in the office, there were water and mountains enough to hike, fish, hunt, snowshoe, cross-country ski or bike someplace different every weekend of the year. Montana was perfect for a fresh start or a second career, when you wanted something slower, or more hands-on. Night and day, Mother Nature came out to party; no wonder so many from California kept heading north to buy land up here. Of course, the locals resented all that attention. Thanks for visiting, the billboards said. Now go back home.

Bedford swirled coffee in the bottom of his mug. He was working late, but did not mind; this new job of his had no regular hours. When needed, he'd work round the clock, having learned long ago to manage with little sleep. But he could also stretch his weekends to four or five days, especially during hunting season. That let Sty guide for a selection of outfitters, which translated into a pile of cash from out-of-state jocks wanting to plunk an elk. Three thousand bucks to wander the Bob Marshall wilderness just for a rack to mount over the mantle? Sty scoffed at these suburban Rambos, but he took their money without hesitation. Life in Montana suited him just fine.

Sty's first career had been more demanding. It started with the military, where a four-year tour turned into twenty before he decided to hang up the uniform. Ten more years as a civilian in the government's vast intelligence community grayed his hair and gave him permanent indigestion; it also kept him poor, so he quit and signed on with a private contractor in the same line of work. Pay was better, and less paperwork, but the travel took its toll; immersion in a world of subterfuge developed trust issues, too. Sty's marriage had disintegrated along with his health, and by his mid-fifties, he was living alone. The kitchen cabinets were mostly empty. His medicine cabinet, mostly full.

One day he shambled out of bed, wandered around the third floor walk-up, and decided to stop hating his life. He took the Metro to his fancy office south of the capitol, turned in his ID, and left a fruit basket with his secretary. Then he pushed through glass doors and stepped out into a rainy day. Sty emptied bank accounts, threw boxes from his apartment into a pickup and drove without a plan, vaguely aimed toward Canada or the sunset. A dozen states and three gallons of coffee later, his truck threw a rod outside Kalispell. Sty took that as a sign to settle in Montana.

Sty had spent a year recuperating in a cabin outside town, with no phone or computer. He ate what he caught and others grew, went to bed early, rose late and filled days with trolling the mountains on foot, or paddling across Flathead. He jogged, and rode a bike into town. The meds dropped off; his beard grew in more salt than pepper. Eventually he got bored, so he bought a few toys and jumped back into cyberspace.

Tucked behind a Coffee Traders corner table one brisk October morning, Sty had been watching the sky through plate glass. The first flakes of snow were falling. His laptop pinged with new email, interrupting an evaluation of the weather. An acquaintance from his past life had written a one-word note—*Job?*—and attached the back half of a phone number. Sty ambled over to the pastry case for a sweet roll, then slid back into the wooden chair at his table. He keyed the rest of the number into his cell from memory.

A woman answered and began her pitch immediately. She was a senior partner in an insurance company whose clients had special needs—paintings, sculpture, artifacts, jewelry and other *objets d'art* that hadn't been purchased from department stores or downtown galleries.

"It's a niche, Bedford," she told him. "We've perched on the edges of a five billion dollar business, where provenance is undocumented." Sty translated as she talked: not the actual black market full of pedigreed masterpieces stolen from museums or archaeological digs that move around and are pursued by international law enforcement agencies; she's talking about the fringes, where items of less certain origin and ownership tend to ebb and flow. More of a gray area, unsupervised and apparently lucrative. The wild west gone global.

The woman was still speaking. "A few of us realized there might be customers wanting an extra layer of security for their holdings. Turns out we were right. We set up shop and now we charge exorbitant rates and promise full recovery. So far, our client list has made our investment worthwhile. In fact, we're shorthanded, which is why I thought of you."

Sty hadn't needed much of a push to sign on. Art theft and recovery had been a particular professional interest, and he still had friends in low places. The work she described seemed easy, the salary handsome, and the legal blowback minimal since official law enforcement preferred to leave this crowd to duke out its own battles. As long as he could manage time zones and had access to an airport, he could live wherever he pleased.

"Resources?" he'd asked. "Assets?"

"An expense account with liberal parameters," his new boss had explained. "You can use or develop other assets as you see fit. Most of us don't have much trouble with that."

With his own network still mostly intact, Sty wasn't worried. "When do I start?"

"I'll email the boilerplate, you fax back the usual stuff. Most important thing about us is this: we don't like to lose anything, but if we do, we're expected to find it." She paused to let the message sink in.

"It's a good job, Bedford, with the kind of drama you'd expect from wealthy, high maintenance clients. They're rich and demanding, people with a veneer of respectability stretched over acres of greed and envy. There's the constant contest, too, for who can have the best, biggest and most. So they guard their stuff jealously while looking for ways to expand their collections. Frankly, some of our work involves having to take back to one client what another has purloined. It can be delicate at times, and requires a combination of baby-sitting and hard-nosed detective work."

Sty wanted to assure her that wouldn't be a problem, but she kept speaking. "That's another reason you came to mind. Your rep as a guy who can get the job done is solid, but I'm also aware of your people skills. You're a good fit for us."

"Thanks," Sty said.

"You're welcome," she said. "Besides, I'm figuring that with people you know, you're likely to generate new business for us, too." She paused. "I'll send a second packet as well, this one by mail. It's old and slow, but snail's still reliable and doesn't leave that nasty electronic trail." Sty nodded. Once this stuff gets in your veins, it never leaves, he thought. You're always cautious, always a little paranoid. "You'll be responsible for a dozen clients; you'll also get a list of folks we're keeping eyes on. Same as always: know the targets, know the threats.

"Contact your clients soon," she said. "Establish rapport." Sty lost the next phrase when a tray of dishes crashed to the floor behind the counter at the end of the room. He glanced over briefly, then snugged the phone to his ear. "Your passport's up to date?"

Sty stifled a laugh. Passport? Which one?

The call had ended after a stroll down memory lane with his new boss. They'd worked a few capers together back in the age of punch cards; they had several mutual acquaintances and a professional admiration for each other's abilities. After tucking the cell into his vest pocket, Sty cut a wedge of cinnamon bun and chewed slowly.

It felt good to be back in the game.

5

The package showed up on the front stoop at his cabin later that week—a manila envelope addressed by hand. Inside, Sty found lists, photographs and contact information. Much of what he was expected to watch over was familiar on account of past experience or more recent dabbling. He recognized several of the clients' names, too, and was faintly surprised now to be working for these people rather than treating them as possible informants or crooks. Sty made appointments and flew first class to check security and pass out his cell phone number.

That had prepared him for the quarterly phone conference with his new boss in December. She began that meeting by asking for reports from each person. Then she talked about the annual bonus, and remarked on how quiet things had been.

"Except for that Latour from the cellar in Dublin, nothing's been stirring for some time," she said. "A welcome break, after this past May and July."

Sty had been studying reports and noticed those bumps. "Any way of accounting for that?" he asked.

"The weather." The call included company agents scattered across several continents, but Bedford didn't recognize this speaker.

A nasal, irritating earnest voice broke in. Stockholm. "These difficulties were in South America and Asia, yes?" Sty found him annoying, particularly when one of the hits the Swede highlighted had been at a house that was now on his own list of responsibilities.

"Let's bear in mind that this is a collaboration, not a contest," his boss said, interrupting the Scandinavian. "We're prepared for ebb and flow as items move around, but we're also building levees and plugging leaks. Whatever the cause, our job is to make sure such trends don't continue. Right, people?"

Murmured assent rose from around the globe.

"Speaking of which, has there been any progress with the Latour?"

Such stratospherically expensive champagne was desirable for bragging rights. It would be brought out at parties to sit in splendor and elicit awe, but other corks were pulled to fill glasses. This bottle, however, had sprouted legs.

"We've got some promising leads," said the agent in Vancouver responsible for their client in Ireland.

"Keep turning over rocks, see what crawls out." After final remarks, Sty's boss wrapped up the meeting with wishes for a prosperous new year.

In March, her tone had been less sanguine. "Different story this time, people," she began. "Given what's going on with our accounts, I've been checking outside the firm to see if we're an aberration. Turns out the loss rate across the boards this past year was definitely above average. It's been gaining steam since November, with a definite uptick this past February."

Sty took notes as she reported on losses suffered by their company or others who had shared information: Oriental jade, letters by Napoleon, a da Vinci sketch, ancient bronzes, assorted gems. Mention of a Fabergé egg brought a chuckle from several: one of those always seemed to be rolling around loose. The places from which these things got pinched varied, too, from Nassau to Kuala Lumpur to Johannesburg and beyond. Then there was the piece taken from a client in his portfolio.

That burglary had occurred in the first week of February, resulting in the disappearance of a carved bowl. The client had insured the piece for far more than its actual value, but Sty supposed that his new firm was glad to collect the premium. When the owner called with the news of its theft, Sty caught a plane to Buenos Aires to check the house and staff. Security was tight, and the turnover of house help about standard. He had little new to report during the conference.

"Other than being part of a general trend, there's not much in common here. Maybe with oil and gold fluctuating, it's just a bull market for stolen artwork," Sty's boss mused. "The hits are far apart and the thief or thieves seem to be after widely different items. Furthermore, he, she or they are managing to hit places with excellent security."

"Inside jobs?" Sty asked immediately. This was often the problem. That, and fraud, where the insured person tried to take the company for a ride.

"No need to rule anything out yet," she said.

"We've had nothing in this sector." Stockholm's nasal voice was not well-suited to cockiness, but the remarks still made Sty's skin crawl.

His boss interjected an icy, "Very well," which silenced further comment from the Nordic agent. She redirected the conversation. "Let's recheck security measures, and then those of you whose clients suffered recent losses should probe deeper for connections."

"Can you send the whole enchilada on what you know up to this point?" Sty asked.

"There's encrypted email going out as we speak."

Sty downloaded the material as the phone meeting continued, arranging data in columns that listed item, place and time. He doodled on page margins as others talked, listening with half an ear to Vancouver's protests against criticism of her efforts investigating the lost bottle of Latour. No theory to explain these events prevailed, and the call ended with promises from each agent regarding diligence and determination.

He'd spent the weekend after the conference hiking snow along trails in Glacier National Park, ruminating on the lists he'd made. Different parts of the world, with a notable exception of the States. Small items, easy to move, with everything worth at least a quarter million. Unless you count the real value of that bowl in Argentina, he corrected himself. Haphazard timing, it seemed, suggesting an unfortunate coincidence of random events.

But Bedford didn't like random, or coincidence. When he returned to his cabin, he reviewed the lists. Since thieves went to where stuff was, he reasoned that place was the least important part of the puzzle. That left the items themselves, and the dates. As he'd seen, the things stolen were of no particular kind—they weren't all paintings, or jewels, or coins. But they were of similar size: no object was bigger than a breadbox. That suggested the crooks didn't need elaborate transportation or packing plans.

The worth of these pieces also showed an element of consistency: nothing valued at more than half a million, and yet each had a book price north of a quarter mill. So, no junk, but also not much of an impact on their clients' bottom lines. These thefts were more of a nuisance than reason to summon the cavalry. The cumulative effect was considerable, but no one person would be overly concerned.

Then Sty checked dates, which was trickier. Owners were lax in their reporting, few inspected all their belongings every day, and many did not pay close attention to particular items. The distractions of the ridiculously rich, Sty mused. What dates they could verify went into the 'Time' column, but the numbers there were only a jumble.

In this line of work, Sty reminded himself, little is random, and there are very few coincidences. He split the 'Time' column into month and day, leaving to one side those burglaries that occurred on a guessed-at date. Only certain months, he noticed. November and February had popped up during the recent phone conference, then July and May when he added data his boss had sent. The list of days gave him an odd set of digits: 17, 29, 5, 23, 11, 2. Sty stared at both of these new columns, seeking a pattern. Nothing random.

He arranged chronologically the list of days on which there had been activity. Then he gave a numerical value to each month, and placed those numbers in two columns: 2, 5, 7, 11 for the months; 2, 5, 11, 17, 23, 29 for the days.

Something about both lists looked familiar. Finally it struck him: They were all prime numbers. Sty checked his data again, examined again what had been lifted, consulted a file that had come with him from Virginia. A faint memory, long dormant, was stirring.

Phine.

Surely not. She was dead, or at least inactive, right? But then, that's what they'd said about a volcano in Central America Sty had toured when he was working the Caribbean. Long after his visit, he had been watching the news and seen pictures of how the volcano that had been quiet for decades had erupted and buried a village with a rockslide.

Deciding the possibility warranted exploration, Bedford made two calls. The first was to an old friend in England. Foxe had a tendency to stroll on either side of a fence, but Sty also knew that if anyone had information regarding the theory beginning to form in his brain, it was likely to be this man across the pond. So he probed, asking about the Brit's current projects.

As expected, Foxe was cagey. But eventually the fellow let on that he was brokering several deals that might have a certain linkage with Bedford's new firm. One of those involved a woman with whom they both had been previously acquainted. That tip gave Sty an iceberg of information.

"Would you keep me apprised?" he'd asked. "My current employer has reason to be intrigued, as do I."

"I'm rather busy," Foxe had grumbled. "It's early spring and my roses need tending."

"And yet, I'd be grateful for your assistance," Sty had said, "as I know you have been grateful for mine." Foxe liked his home south of London, so leaving it would require this additional pressure. Sty had been instrumental in extricating Foxe from Poland in the days leading up to Walesa's rebellion.

"You needn't play that card, old man," Foxe had replied. Five thousand miles away, Sty could picture the pinched face. He chuckled.

His next call had gone to Madrid, where a different friend staffed the concierge desk at a hotel favored by tourists with more money than brains. Dulcinea, a Filipina he'd worked with in his past life, was resourceful; she also had a large family.

"You'll remember stories I've told about a woman who had eluded me over the years," Sty began. "Any chance you've heard in the past year or two of someone fitting her description?"

"*Señor*," Dulcinea began, "It is strange you ask me that now. I remembered our conversations about this woman when a few months ago I heard of someone who sounded like her. Following a most discreet investigation, I learned that this person is almost certainly a collector. Not only that, but she appears to be working with another mutual friend of ours. The Frenchman?" Dulcinea's voice rose slightly at the mention of this second person.

"Ah, the Frenchman," Sty repeated. His mind was churning. "Did you learn anything else?"

"Only that this woman has a flat in Portugal, near the sea. It is very dusty there."

"Dusty?" Sty said, puzzled.

"*Sí, señor*. But my niece, she makes an excellent maid."

6

The second quarter's phone conference had taken place in early May, six weeks ahead of schedule. Sty took the evening call at the Eureka, in his corner office on the third floor.

The Eureka was one of Kalispell's oldest hotels, built when the town was little more than a wide spot in the road. Early on, it welcomed travelers dropped off by the train or looking for adventure. As the town grew, it held tourists and speculators. Soon, the hotel was a quaint throwback to frontier ways, eclipsed by newer, fancier places that boasted heated pools and skylit terrariums.

Sty had stumbled across the Eureka his first day in Kalispell. He'd arrived in a wrecker, after his pickup left him stranded at a cherry stand near Flathead Lake. The tow truck's driver had dropped him at a shop where the mechanic was rebuilding a snow machine's carburetor. Sty left the keys and went for a stroll, ending up in front of the Eureka's plate glass window.

The *For Sale* sign caught him. Inside he found dark lacquered paneling in the lobby and anterooms, carved railings for the staircase, brass fixtures, brocade draperies, and carpets. Sty had a soft spot for antiques, but too much on his mind to think seriously about buying the place.

A few days later, with a local realtor's help, Sty found a cabin with a view of the Lake where he could unpack and detox. Weeks passed, and gradually his health improved. For the first time in years he could take a deep breath without hacking or feeling a twinge.

But it was slow, this life, and during a trip into town for ammo and grapefruit, he drove by the Eureka to take another look. Seeing the sign still there, he called. The owner gave him an earful about resort communities, Montana real estate, and the general backwardness of living out west as opposed to back east. A week later, after more calls, Sty bought the place for a song.

He had the brass work cleaned, but kept the floral carpet, despite its thin patches. Threadbare in the cause of preserving authenticity was an easy choice. But a few changes were necessary. First, Sty priced rooms below market in an effort to turn the hotel's bottom line black. Then he hired a local contractor who'd been laid off to manage the place. That left Sty free to come and go as he pleased.

Next, Sty commandeered a pair of top story rooms for his office, knocking out the dividing wall and converting the second bath into a kitchenette. He used the place often because he liked sounds of life nearby even late at night. It was an added bonus that nobody could get to him very easily here. Safe and secure: watchwords for his life.

"We're noticing a definite trend, people." Sty's boss got off to a quick start. "Some person or group is eating our lunch and not leaving crumbs." She went on to recount how insured losses over the past twelve months now approached nine million dollars, which was sizeable for their company. "We've got deep pockets," she said, "But I don't need to tell you that we're not interested in this sort of bleeding." She went on to remind them of company policy regarding recovery or remuneration.

Murmurs of assent came through Sty's speakerphone until the distinctive nasal voice of Stockholm cut in.

"Do we need to focus on particular problem areas? Because, as I have mentioned before, there have been no difficulties to speak of in my remit."

Sty wished he could reach through the line and throttle the twerp, but his boss intervened. "Let me be clear. Whereas each of you has specific regions and clients, we must work together against a threat of this nature." Her voice became less stern. "That's why I've asked Kalispell to outline a theory he has. Proceed."

Forcing calm into his voice, Sty spent the next quarter hour walking the group through the patterns he'd noticed, sharing the intel he'd collected. Then he explained why that led him to suspect the activity of an old nemesis.

"It appears you are putting a great deal of weight on these prime numbers," Vancouver said. Sty liked her smoky voice, and didn't mind a thoughtful challenge.

"The primes are just part of a bigger picture," Sty said.

He'd briefed his boss on his run-ins with Josephine, admitting that he hadn't considered her to be a factor until he had connected this set of dots. "I thought she was dead," Bedford had told the woman in New York, "or at least retired. But she may be up to her old tricks." His suspicions were enough to encourage his boss to press him for closer attention to this mysterious person from Bedford's past.

"Every seven years she throws a birthday party, and in the year leading up to that, Phine goes on a shopping spree," Sty explained during the conference call. "According to my files, we're in the seventh year. Actually, it's the seventh seven for her. In the past, she's collected gifts for all the guests she invites. Expensive gifts. I expect that this year, on account of the juxtaposition of sevens, she plans to go all out."

"She travels the globe in search of such items and pinches them from well-protected homes?" This from Tokyo, whose accented tenor sounded rather touchy.

"No," Sty said. "She hires people for that."

"And you know these people?" asked Stockholm.

"Again, no. But I know someone who does."

His boss cut in. "While I am not yet persuaded this Josephine Wainwright is our only legitimate culprit, I am sufficiently convinced that she warrants additional scrutiny. Kalispell, I want you to continue with that, and to keep us informed." After repeating the date of the group's next meeting, she brought the conversation to a close.

Sty would have his hands full. Operations were never easy, and few went smoothly, but with Phine in the mix, the variables increased significantly. He spun in his chair to face a window. His contacts in Europe would prove invaluable, but they would also be insufficient. Sty needed more help.

Exactly how much and of what sort would become more clear as he amassed data, but for now, the next step was obvious. He needed someone nimble, smart enough to read the tea leaves, a person he could trust. Sty scanned a mental list, filed a name for later use, and smiled. He rose from the chair, cracked the knuckles on both hands, and stared into the night sky. Then he pulled his phone from a pocket and set wheels in motion that, some days hence, would send Max speeding down a Michigan highway.

The cell phone chimed with an incoming text: his nephew had arrived in Grand Rapids. Bedford tapped a quick reply before wheeling to his computer for a file to send. Max could print it at the hotel.

Kid's a quick study, Sty thought—but he had known this for years. Even when Max was in high school, Sty had thrown him an occasional bone because the boy showed promise, which made his uncle proud. After Max dropped out of college, Sty offered him steady work. Taught him some of the craft, too, and found the kid a natural.

With the file Sty sent, Max would have plenty to work with. Much of the information in it had come from Foxe, whom Sty had squeezed hard once he'd decided to chase Phine. The Brit had explained, reluctantly, that his new employer preferred elaborate plans and procedures, like couriers with photographs of specific items she desired. Foxe hinted that he'd been involved in the process.

Couriers and photographs? Sty had been incredulous at these old school touches. Eminently more secure, Foxe had said. Yeah, thought Sty, as long as they don't get intercepted by, say, some homeless guy at the airport.

Max had been aces with that Dutch student, managing to grab the briefcase with its pictures. By comparing these to images from his company's files, Bedford had found two matches: an ornate fountain pen and a Bach manuscript that had several years earlier been discovered, only to vanish from the public eye and begin circulating very quietly among private collectors. Max's third picture showed an item Sty's firm did not insure, but one of great value nevertheless. It was a baseball card, which both amused and puzzled Sty.

He'd seen firsthand Phine's eclectic tastes, but figured they were also more refined. Sports heroes on cardboard just wasn't her style, so why was a photo of the famous Yankee traveling with de Groot? He'd solve that later; what mattered was that Phine was now a live target.

Sty pulled another pair of photographs from a folder that was gaining heft. Max had sent one of these after getting it from a contact of his own that he was cultivating. Sty had taught Max this, that the flow of information was vital, and that pieces of data which made no sense in one context often turned out to be essential in another. It was a grainy print, enlarged to highlight a slender, balding man, slightly turned from the camera.

A distinctively sharp nose stood out, as did the shading of a mole on the right cheek. Sty set this photo next to an image forwarded by Dulcinea, by way of her niece's cell phone. It showed a young man and woman standing in front of the Eiffel tower. The woman wore sunglasses and a floppy straw hat, but Sty would have recognized Phine in a burkha. Her thin companion had dark, bushy hair and a wide smile. Sharp nose, mole on his right cheek.

After scribbling some notes, Sty pushed the folder aside. He tossed a pot pie in the microwave and cracked a beer from the mini-fridge to accompany supper at his desk while assembling Max's packet. Scans of the photos along with detailed notes went into an attachment Sty encrypted and sent.

If his calculations were correct, they had about a month to thwart thefts that would certainly be attempted, and to recover a cache of already stolen goods. From experience Sty knew about Josephine's legendary parties: she would scatter or destroy her dubiously acquired trinkets, and then go to ground. The window of opportunity was tiny. To keep his job, to say nothing of preserving his reputation, he'd have to be both lucky and good.

Cumin sat across from Trevor on the molded plastic bench seat, his head in his hands.

"This is depressing."

Trevor, waiting for the man next to him to elucidate, carefully brushed animal hair from his trousers. The next vehicle he stole would not belong to a pet owner.

When Mr. Cumin failed to comment further, Trevor spoke. "We can't do anything more until the flight arrives, correct?" he asked. It was distressing to see his employer in this state. Trevor had hoped activity might distract him. Instead, the older man seemed to be sinking into a slough of despond.

More silence. Then Mr. Cumin lifted his head slowly. "Do you like this sort of work, Trevor?"

Trevor plucked a coarse white hair from his coat sleeve. "Mr. Cumin, that's like asking a philologist if he finds diphthongs interesting. This is work I was made to do. I derive deep satisfaction from it."

Cumin nodded and peered at the floor.

"Are those any better?" Trevor asked, pointing at the other man's shoes.

"In terms of size or fashion?" Cumin asked.

Trevor shrugged and then stood, palming the marbled chunk of plastic.

"Aren't your fingers meant to go *in* the holes?" Cumin asked.

"They're not large enough." Trevor stepped on to the hardwood surface and walked to the line painted on the floor.

Cumin pointed at the maple-planked lanes. "You're to roll the bloody thing, not throw it."

The wide man acknowledged the comment with a tip of his head. He took Mr. Cumin's sarcasm as a sign of managed disappointment. Turning, Trevor narrowed his eyes to slits, calculating distance and estimating velocity. He passed the ball from hand to hand like it was a dinner bun. Back home he threw what the Yanks would call telephone poles; in comparison, what he held now was a feather. He could hit the center of any outside pin down there ten times out of ten without it ever touching the floor. But not tonight. No need to attract attention.

Trevor stood at the line, brought his left arm back and sent his ball into the gutter.

7

Van Dorman High was on the south side of Holland. Max pulled into the parking lot at the bottom of the third inning and bought a hot dog from the boosters club. Inside the gate, he took a bite and threw the rest into an overflowing garbage can closer to the stands.

For late spring in Michigan, it was downright hot; the cheap navy overcoat made him sweat. Max adjusted the horn-rimmed glasses and tugged at the fedora that completed the outfit he had bought at a thrift store that morning. He gently brushed back the hair above his ears and felt the shortened sideburns. Graying powder stuck to his fingers.

Max banged up metal steps, turned right, then climbed to the top of the bleachers. The home crowd was thin, especially this far up; too many other options beckoned on such a fine day. He threaded his way to the end of the row of seats and then down a few steps to stand behind a clump of spectators.

"Mr. de Groot?" he called out.

A half dozen heads turned at the name.

"Pieter de Groot?"

Only two this time, and Max ignored the bald fellow. The other de Groot was his tall student from the airport.

"A word with you, sir?" he said.

Pieter de Groot leaned toward the woman next to him to whisper and then stood. He worked his way along the row and walked up to meet Max.

"Let's talk up there," Max motioned toward the empty top row. "After you."

De Groot climbed the remaining steps without protest and took a seat on the warm aluminum. Max followed but remained standing. Glaring at de Groot, he reached inside his coat for a notepad.

"Mr. de Groot," he said. "You have lately arrived in this country for purposes yet unknown. We have a few questions about your travels."

Pieter was having trouble swallowing. The bruises on his left cheek were still noticeable; a cut there had been stitched. He had told his cousin in Holland that this was the result of a fall he'd taken before leaving Italy. She had been sympathetic. Now he put a hand to his face in an effort to hide the marks.

"Yes, I did come to here, but only for visiting relatives." He stopped, and then peered back at Max. "One moment. Who did you say you were?"

"What matters is not who I am, but what you have done," Max said. He flipped open the notebook, and recited details from the blank first page. "Departed Archibaldo da Vinci airport in Rome, three nights ago, cleared customs at JFK, then on to Baltimore. One suitcase, black."

Pieter's mouth hung open. How did this man know so much? Who else had information about his life? He was boring, no one important, a mere student who had never dreamed that a simple act of greed could result in so much unhappiness. Next time he would be more disciplined. But that Frenchman had been so persuasive and accommodating. Of course Pieter could stop and see his aunt who lived so near Baltimore, the little man had promised. In fact, Baltimore was exactly where Pieter would meet those who wanted the briefcase he would carry. The job proposed by this Frenchman had seemed so facile. It should have worked to my advantage, Pieter thought. But I am always so unlucky.

"A scuffle ensued after you landed," Max continued, consulting his notebook. "In Baltimore." He peered over the top of his glasses. Then reaching into his coat once more, he said, "This was turned in to airport security." He tossed a leather wallet at the young man. "Does it look familiar?"

"My wallet! I lost—" de Groot looked at Max. Should he tell this odd person everything that had occurred, how he had been taken while trying to find the house of his aunt and beaten in an old warehouse nearby, only to be abandoned there? How he had managed to free himself, stumble outside, persuade a kindly stranger to use a cell phone and call his aunt? How he had lied to her about losing his wallet, and pleaded with her to purchase a ticket for him to continue his journey to Michigan to see other relatives? How he planned to pay her back as soon as he got home, and how he would never under any circumstance carry luggage for criminals?

Pieter de Groot composed himself and slid the wallet into his jeans. "Thank you," he said.

Max's eyes narrowed as he leaned toward the young man. All he wanted was confirmation that Collingsworth was involved. With Uncle Sty's help he'd stop this rash of robberies; on his own, he'd see that this Dutchman got compensated for what he'd experienced. First, though, he needed to make sure he was on the right track.

"Was this the man who took you to the warehouse?" Max showed Pieter a photo of a Pennsylvania state senator.

"No."

"This?" Max handed over an image of his previous university's provost, lifted from the school's webpage.

De Groot shook his head.

"What about this?" Max held out a copy of the grainy picture he'd received from Sharon Palmetter, whom Max had met during his second year of college. He had switched his major to criminal justice long enough to wrangle an internship in a Philadelphia office of the FBI where Sharon, an administrative assistant in the records department, had taken him under her wing and introduced him to several agents. They were all eager to help the college kid who wanted to know everything about everything. When he left, Sharon kept in touch through email, hoping Max might yet want to meet her daughter.

She had sent him the photo of R. Stayber Collingsworth that had been circulating among law enforcement agencies. To date, nothing specific had been pinned on Collingsworth, but his activities had raised the eyebrows of those who knew of the man's interests in art and proclivities toward theft. When he had entered the States last month, the picture popped up on the alert lists.

It was the sort of notice Sharon knew Max liked to see; she sent it with an invitation to a picnic she was planning. Max had begged off with the flu, but kept the picture. He in turn passed it along to his uncle, just in case. According to the email Max had retrieved at the hotel that morning, his hunch had paid off.

Pieter de Groot held the photo Max gave him. His hand shook and he handed it back.

"That's Henri Courvoisier," Max said. "An arms dealer from France."

"French?" de Groot asked. "He sounded English to me. Perhaps I did not see properly. May I look again?"

"Certainly."

De Groot studied the picture. The only Frenchman he had met during this entire ordeal had been that oily reptile Renard, at that pub in Venice. Renard, who had promised easy money for carrying a briefcase to America, where Pieter would visit his aunt who lived near Baltimore, before traveling to his relatives in Michigan, and on to sightseeing in Los Angeles. But he had lost the case, which meant he would not receive the money he had been promised. No California either, he thought morosely. Only this dreadful baseball on a very hot day.

"Yes. I am certain this is the man." He handed the picture back to Max. "But he was definitely British. His companion as well."

"There were two of them, then?"

The student nodded. "The other man was not tall, but very powerful." Not very tall for a Dutchman meant something like six-one, Max thought. "He did this to me." Pieter took away the hand that had covered his cheek.

"What was it you brought for this man, Mr. de Groot?"

"A briefcase only. But I saw nothing of what was inside."

"Indeed. Well, Mr. de Groot, you have been very helpful. I will be sure to notify the proper authorities as to your assistance in this matter. However, I must also ask you to remain silent about what has transpired, as it may compromise an ongoing investigation. I will also caution you against any similar foolish behavior in the future."

The young man hung his head. "Of course. It was stupid of me to assume this would end well, but the money was appealing. As you say, I have learned my lesson and I will never attempt such a thing again. I very much appreciate your discretion, Mr.—" His head came up in search of a name, but he was speaking only to air.

8

In a spacious flat south of the Rua Doctor José de Matos, a setting sun turned the penthouse trophy room to amber. Standing next to a creamy leather sofa, a petite woman held a crystal champagne flute. She sipped, then set the delicate glass on an end table of burled walnut. Her fingers now free, she plucked macadamias from the outstretched hand of a bronze shepherd that had once been part of the clock tower in Basel.

The Mediterranean and Atlantic merged outside her window, both oceans fusing into swirls of azure, cobalt and turquoise from this height and distance. She marveled at the panoply of color, delighted by the shifting, brilliant array of an ocean alive at her fingertips. Was there any rival to the glory she witnessed through her windows every day?

This room's palette complimented those hues with warm earth tones that ranged from sand to chocolate on fabrics and furniture. Prized possessions nestled on shelves and hung from textured walls, drawing the eye gently from point to point. The collection was expanding in a most satisfying way as the day of her party drew nearer.

Seven years, she thought with a start. And I have been doing this since.... She did not finish the sentence. But as always, she was pleased with the sense of order and purpose her life now exhibited, and with the way preparations for this year's festivities were proceeding. She twirled slowly to take in the room's nooks and crannies, pausing to admire objects that spoke to her, sang to her, shone for her.

The obvious exception was that confounded Russian egg, glaring from a tripod on the brass mantle that had been liberated from a Parisian *arrondissement*. Its fussy complexity and patent showmanship did not fit with her décor. She fought the urge to scream by rehearsing her purpose for possession of it: to snub the face-lifted wife of that stuffy Bulgarian software 'genius'. The insufferable couple would receive this egg as a gift at her party. Each of her guests would be given a present of true value and lasting beauty, but this egg was different. As anyone who owned certain treasures understood, high profile items were double-edged. The irony assuaged her.

She retreated to her *sanctum sanctorum* each day at this time, to meditate. So long as her portion of southern Portugal stayed off the lists of popular destinations, she would continue to spend as much time as possible in this enclave at the tip of Faro. She favored such coastal apartments, having been raised near the sea. But she insisted on places that boasted splendid weather, in contrast to the dreary land of her birth. She had fled that island far to the north while still young, and was glad to be rid of its endless gray drizzle. Daily sunshine in a quiet spot, where the produce was fresh and the smells of Africa so very near, brought life.

Josephine Wainwright needed the serenity of her surroundings especially now, given how near that twit she relied on was to spoiling her birthday fête. Such a simple errand she had sent him on: all she required was for him to procure items essential for poetry and music. When one held a party only every seven years, one needed to have one's surroundings appropriately sublime; surely he could grasp that truth. There were permissible exceptions, of course, to this sublimity—like the egg, which she would tolerate for the delicious sensation of foisting it on that boorish woman. Otherwise, she preferred the tranquility of understatement.

One with questionable tact might, therefore, have pointed out the incongruity of the card she planned to give away, but here she had devised an equally adept rationalization. She had invited a person outside her typical circle of acquaintance and wanted him to feel welcomed. What better way of extending hospitality toward a newly retired team manager than to present him with a memento from the sport he had recently left, and from which he had made such a handsome fortune through opportunely placed wagers? While the object itself was vulgar in the extreme, it served, in Josephine's opinion, as a fitting tribute. It would honor his attendance at this, her seventh party. It would also demonstrate in a wonderfully subtle way the extent of her reach, which was important for those who sought to expand their own collections.

But now all was in jeopardy with that nitwit's ineptitude. The thought of cancelling or postponing her party was out of the question. He would simply have to deliver. Josephine's brow furrowed. She was unwilling to imagine an outcome different from the one she had already designed. Her pulse quickened, her stomach knotted. Ruination lay perilously near.

A sip of champagne soothed her frayed nerves, upset not twenty four hours ago by the insufferable man's contentious pleading. She glanced at the bottle, gently swathed and nestled in ice. Its fine layer of dust—the only dust she allowed in this pristine room—had not been disturbed with the cork's removal. This further evidence of Chesa's care calmed the woman, and caused her to reflect on a suitable bonus for the girl, given such attention to detail. A pin, perhaps. Something silver.

Then her mood shifted again, darkening at the thought of her lackey's losing the courier's briefcase. Her quality of life would suffer on account of that idiot's carelessness; he had put the very essence of her carefully laid plans at risk. Refusing to trust electronic conveyance, she insisted on hand delivery of vital information, and so routinely used people to deliver sensitive information—one to transport a list of names and addresses, another to convey photographs of the items to be procured.

When had that perfect plan ever gone awry? Had any of the others experienced trouble with this method? The dolt was not dependable, had not been since those days in the circus. Why had she deigned, even in her youth, to marry such a fool?

Josephine upbraided herself a minute more, wanting to enforce resolve. Then she lifted a gleaming bell from the table and rang it. Gold striking platinum made a pleasing sound.

The doorway darkened with the arrival of a maid. "Yes, Miss Wainwright?"

"Chesa, I'll take dinner on the terrace."

"Very good, madam. The usual time?"

"Of course."

Chesa Areglo, an emigrant from Manila, turned to leave.

"Chesa?" the older woman called.

"Yes, madam?"

"You made the delivery to that French person?"

"Yes, madam, this morning, as you instructed."

"Very good. Do fill this glass before you go." She nodded toward the half-empty flute on the side table, and watched the girl carefully extract the large bottle from a dimpled steel ice bucket. Latour was a personal favorite, and Josephine drank it often in this room. Why have such fine things if not to enjoy them? Pity the fools who collected wines like this only to store them in cellars and bring them out on occasion to impress friends. Josephine received the glass from Chesa, admiring the honey-colored liquid and tiny bubbles through a scrim of condensation.

"I shall never be able to finish the magnum alone, Chesa. Please fill poor Baskerville's bowl as well." She glanced at the greyhound curled by the window in a pool of sunlight. "He looks so parched."

"Right away, Miss Wainwright."

9

"How can you be so sure about July seventh?" Max asked his uncle.

They were talking by phone after Max's trip to Michigan; now Max was at his desk going over the case notes Sty had sent by email.

"It's a prime number," Sty said. "Actually, a double prime, with July being the seventh month and that day, the seventh, another prime. A quadruple prime, if you factor in that this is her seventh seven-year party. Irresistible."

Bedford could not see the puzzled face of Max, but figured the boy needed further explication. "Just like prime numbers are among the most unusual digits, this woman thinks she is similarly unique, and mysterious," he added.

"Which you know because—?" Max asked.

"We both started in this business about the same time, albeit on different sides of the law, and she was in my sights long enough for a close look. I thought her ship had sailed a while back, but apparently I was wrong. Now that she's active again, I don't want to underestimate her. She's trouble, Max, and these days, I'm all about nice and easy." He chuckled. "But I will admit, this woman can throw one fine party."

"Sounds like the voice of experience."

Max's uncle fingered the cylinder on his desk. Venetian glass, eighteenth century, museum quality; worth three months of an army captain's salary. Thirty-odd years ago, he'd slipped into her place in Barbados primed for an easy arrest, but to his surprise, the rooms were thick with Congressmen and South American warlords. He'd taken Phine aside and showed her the warrant, which she'd dismissed with a wave.

"I couldn't possibly leave my guests—that simply would not be polite. But as you've gone to so much trouble to find me, do accept this token as a memento." She'd tossed him the cylinder like it was a can of soda. "A present for you," she'd said. "On my birthday." Her smile nearly made him forget why he'd come. "This is only my second party, so I'm still deciding what sort of people to invite. If you'd been on my guest list, I'd have put something more substantial aside. But as it is, this will have to suffice." With that, she'd melted into a clutch of revelers on the patio, leaving him behind and bewildered. His backup was insufficient for this crowd; he'd quit the place clumsily, tail between legs.

Sty should have reported the gift. But the piece intrigued him, almost as much as the woman who'd thrown it. He promised himself he'd set things to rights in his next encounter with this mysterious woman, but years passed without Josephine making a peep. Sty got busy chasing other thieves and she sank to the bottom of a tall pile.

News of her party in Monaco reached him just days before the event and he rushed down with high hopes. That had been another disaster, one which nearly ended his life. Years passed before he got a tip about another of Josephine's soirées, but he arrived late and found nothing other than rubble in her wake. And that had been the pattern: he'd hear distant rumblings about her antics but reports were so infrequent that Sty couldn't justify tasking precious resources for chasing a ghost who only surfaced occasionally. Predictably, Sty now realized with the benefit of hindsight and closer study of the data. Every seven years.

This time, the situation had changed. With his current job, Sty had the luxury of concentrating on a narrow field instead of having to scan multiple horizons. And whether Josephine realized it or not, this time she had raised the stakes by walking into his backyard and directly threatening his livelihood.

Max's voice interrupted his thoughts. "Did you get anything more on that photo I sent you? It sure seemed to light up de Groot."

Bedford shook his head to reenter the present; he shuffled through his folder. "Yeah. Dovetails with info from a contact in France. Looks like Collingsworth could be our man. Turns out he's part of Josephine's stable, one of her top choices when it comes to this sort of work. The prevailing theory is that he's a player on the second tier of art thieves."

"Never made the big time?"

"Don't knock it. If you're top dog, someone's always gunning for you. A collar for the cops means a gold star on their records, and peers are just eager to push anybody off the mountain. But if you're OK with being further down the line—"

Max finished the sentence, seeing what had been invisible. "You can manage a pretty nice life."

"Bingo," Sty said. "This Collingsworth, or what-ever he's calling himself these days, has never been to jail, never been caught at the scene."

"But what's his link to your crazy girlfriend?" Max asked.

"Get this. Back in the day, they were both in the circus—he was a magician and she was an acrobat. They got married, which lasted about fifteen minutes before she walked out on him. I guess even then she'd set her sights on a better life."

"But he still works for her?"

"Maybe he's a romantic," Sty said. "Stranger things have happened. When your heart gets tangled up by love, you're likely to try all kinds of weird stuff."

"Remind me not to ask you for marriage counsel-ing," Max said.

"This an announcement?" his uncle asked.

"Can we stay on task?" Max replied.

Sty chuckled. "You bet. Listen, we caught a cou-ple of breaks. With de Groot's confirmation, we know who we're looking for. The pictures you nabbed tell us what he's after, too. We can narrow down the where with my files, and after studying all we've gathered on this caper, we have a good idea of when he'll hit." Bedford was referring to the lists he'd made, the col-umns that showed what happened when. The increase in action on dates that were prime numbers was, he surmised, not a coincidence. Josephine required her minions to steal only on such days.

"Since we know he's already in the neighbor-hood, and that he has to be done by November, it seems likely that he's planning to work somewhere in the region of Baltimore during July. June's no good—

not a prime numbered month—and neither is August or September. So it's July. As to the seventh, well, like I said. Irresistible.

"That works to our favor, improves our chances of shutting him down and recovering the goods before he blows town. But," Max could hear his uncle tapping the desk. "It's still bugging me how he manages to get in and gone without being seen. I've been to houses that got hit, and the security is first rate. Assuming it was him, I still haven't figured out how he does it. If we don't get smarter fast, come July seventh, we're gonna have a mess on our hands."

"Uncle Sty?" Max's voice was tentative. "What if he doesn't wait for a house to be empty? I mean, what if he just waltzes in when it's full of people?"

Bedford pulled a pencil from the glass cylinder and tested the point with a finger. "Hmm," he said. "Where did you get this bad idea?"

"It's a theory I'm working on," Max said, speaking more quickly now. "According to the notes you sent, on the day of any given robbery, there have been people all over the place—a party, house help, deliveries, groundskeepers, a book group, veterinarians. Besides, if you're right about Josephine being the mastermind, then she's putting Collingsworth on a clock so that he has to lift stuff from all over; he wouldn't have time to learn about the security at each site. Plus, those measures are designed to work when the house is empty or quiet—like at night, or on the weekends, when the owners are away."

"But if people are coming and going—"

"—owners wouldn't turn on the alarms," Max finished.

"So he just blends in, polar bear in a snow storm?"

Max slowed down; he knew he was on the right track. "Or he's a water park in the Mojave. But either way, I'm guessing he uses some sort of diversion. Then when people are looking at one thing, he moves in the opposite direction and presto! He's got what he came for and in the confusion it's not even noticed until the next time the security system is activated. By then, he's long gone."

"Kid, you might be on to something," Sty said. He scrawled a note on the bottom of a page from the file. "So how does that help us with July seven?"

"Been thinking about that," Max said, temporarily shelving his suspicions about the date on which his uncle was fixated. "Got an idea straight from Montana. We need a box canyon."

From the photos in Pieter de Groot's briefcase, Max's uncle determined that two of Collingsworth's three targets were insured by his new firm: a Bach manuscript and a fountain pen from the early twentieth century. As Sty's files showed, the owners of both lived within fifty miles of Baltimore Washington International airport, which explained why Pieter de Groot had been the mule: someone in Collingsworth's network had discovered that the astronomy student had relatives in the area and enlisted his services in exchange for a free trip.

Max had gone to the airport for that briefcase, tipped off by one his uncle's sources. But at the time, Max hadn't considered how much that source and Collingsworth knew about de Groot, or why. Instead, he concentrated on grabbing what the Dutch student carried. Max knew his antics had slowed the thief down somewhat, but the Brit would find a way to get copies of what he needed. He'd be more cautious, but not deterred from his mission. If Max's theory was right, Collingsworth would spend several days casing the joints he planned to visit. Once he figured out who came and went, Collingsworth would find a way in.

That left the third item on Josephine's list. Sty recognized from the final photograph what Collingsworth was expected to retrieve, and knew his firm didn't hold the policy. At the same time, he was curious, since this piece was so different from the others. For Max, sitting at his desk on the other side of the country, that third photo—an image of George Herman 'Babe' Ruth's rookie card—made him smile. It represented an opportunity. He and uncle Sty could use this card to catch their thief.

Max had special connections with Ruth's rookie card. First, he had been trading baseball cards since middle school, and understood what made collectors gasp. He knew, for instance, that of the dozen or so of the Ruths known to be in existence, there was also an owner in Philadelphia who had recently put the card on display during a baseball memorabilia convention there. Second, as a fan living near Baltimore all his life, he had a proprietary claim: George Herman had started his legendary career just down the road. And third, Max had given one to Orange.

The idea for this gift had started with a shared zeal for baseball between two boys who grew up together; they had a special fascination with the Baltimore Orioles, their local team. Max had started his card collection with a shoebox his father had tucked away in the attic, and through shrewd trading had wound up with several Oriole rookie cards. As the end of high school approached, he decided to give the set to Orange. His graduation gift got exponentially better, though, the day he found that car.

Max had already recovered a few stolen cars, thanks to Troy Kent, a high school dropout who never left town. Most thought him dangerous or irrelevant, but Max listened, and learned. One lesson had come from Troy's bragging about guys who hotwired cars in the parking lots of bars at the edge of town, drove off, and then abandoned them in the woods. Max cashed in on that by locating such cars and collecting rewards offered by the insurance companies.

Once, Troy was on about a poker game. "All this cash on the table, empties all over, people passed out on the floor. It's two, three in the morning. Four guys are playin', then three, then two and the pile keeps growing. One guy calls, raises—more than the other guy has with him. Then the second guy whips out this silver case and opens it." Troy surveyed those clustered around him.

"Inside, it's Babe Ruth," Troy said.

"The baseball card?" someone asked.

"No, his left hand. Of course it was the card, you moron."

Low whistles came from Troy's audience, and a lone voice. "There's only like a hunnerd of those."

"Eleven," Max had corrected the speaker. "Maybe twelve."

Troy looked at Max and then the others. "It was Ruth for sure," he said. "His rookie card."

Total silence.

"He drops it, the other guy calls and they lay down. Guy with the Ruth card loses, three Jacks to an inside straight. Other guy picks up the cash and puts the card back in the case, takes everything out to his car. We think he's gone, but he comes back in, says last round's on him. After we're done, we're all outside ready to split, and this guy starts yelling his head off 'cause he can't find his car." Troy smirked. "Somebody boosted his ride."

The kids around Troy laughed and punched each other. "No way," more than one said.

Max inched closer to Troy. "When did this happen?" he asked.

"Couple weeks, a month, ago."

"Anybody find the car?"

Troy snorted. "Sayonara, baby. Long gone."

But eventually Max turned it up, after searching every back road within forty miles of that bar. He and Orange never managed to locate the owner. The case deep in the car's trunk had protected the Sultan of Swat's first-year smile and, with that card, Max completed the gift for his friend: five Oriole rookies, mounted behind glass, and framed using wood from one of Ripken's broken bats.

The card had been part of Orange's belongings ever since; Max had seen the display hung at the end of the second floor hallway when he had visited that week before their friendship ended. At the time he gave it, Max had no idea how valuable that card would become, but even after he started paying attention, he never thought to ask for it back.

Until today.

Neither Max nor Orange had made noise about it; it was their private joke. For that reason, Max was sure Collingsworth didn't know about the card he'd found back in high school. The thief would target the collector in Philadelphia, not Orange.

Max could use that.

10

Mr. Cumin carefully stored in a separate compartment of his brain the likelihood that another person or group was interested in the items which interested him. Then he gave the remainder of his attention to the necessary ordeal of gathering information. Josephine's targets fell within a triangle with sides no longer than a hundred miles, which made the acquisition of all three on one day technically possible. Cumin would have preferred that, in order to escape this bedeviled continent all the more quickly.

However, as he and Trevor drove from one site to the next, Cumin realized that bottlenecks caused by bridges and tunnels made traffic too unpredictable. He would need to spread the jobs over a two-day period. Preferable, of course, was to have two acceptable days close together. Acceptable days. Cumin sighed.

But as an incurable romantic, he was helpless before his employer's demands. Cumin knew that about himself, just as he knew he would do Josephine's bidding no matter how outlandish. If only certain days of certain months were acceptable to her for the work he did, so be it. Indeed, during his many years of service, her idiosyncratic methods had been completely successful. Why worry now?

He gazed through the windscreen. Trevor and he were sitting at the curb in their silver minivan, an upgrade the former had secured after abandoning the horrible blue van commandeered for his interview with the Dutch graduate student. Cumin's face clouded at portents from that encounter, but he renewed his resolve to trust Josephine's instincts and not rely on self-generated perturbations.

The rambling house Cumin was inspecting this morning resembled others dotting the surrounding landscape. One wing of this estate pushed out into gardens, its glass wall ensuring a commanding view. The conservatory, Cumin surmised. Training binoculars on the front entrance, he spotted a discreet white rectangle in a window adjacent to the door. A notice for the home's security service. How quaint. A low stone wall surrounded the estate's perimeter; the driveway had a gate but no guard.

"Coffee, Mr. Cumin?" Trevor asked, pulling a thermos from between the front seats.

"You know I prefer tea, Trevor," Cumin replied. He continued scanning the grounds for cameras or other indications of challenge.

"Of course, Mr. Cumin. But seeing as we're in the colonies, where a proper cup is unlikely, I thought I might suggest an alternative."

Cumin, displeased, was silent. Yet another reason to detest this country. He traveled here as little as possible, preferring to apply his expertise in other lands. There was too much about these States to dislike, with their garish advertisements attached to any available surface and the execrable manners exhibited by every citizen. The food was ghastly as well. When was the last time he'd had satisfactory mutton? Why did no establishment know how to stew tomatoes for breakfast? How could one be expected to begin one's day with 'waffles'? The very word turned his stomach.

Trevor poured from a flask into a plastic cup, but rather than a bracing dark roast, Cumin noticed an aroma more common to a bakery. "Is that cinnamon, Trevor?" he asked.

The massive man grinned. "Would you believe this bloke's company produces fourteen different flavors of coffee?" He gestured toward the mansion they were watching. "The market I visited last evening had the full display." he said. "I purchased a packet of each, for the sake of comparison." He sipped, and sighed. "Lovely."

Trevor reached into the seat behind him to slice the plastic around a large cardboard box. "I've also bought a flat of scones, Mr. Cumin. A dozen each of blueberry, orange-cranberry-walnut and chocolate. Would you care for one?"

Cumin suppressed an oath, turning his attention to a folded sheet of paper that he withdrew from his coat pocket. He ran his finger down the printed columns. Although he had memorized the information there, he took great comfort in rehearsing what he knew. Practice, practice, practice was Cumin's motto, a holdover from his days in the circus, where he'd left nothing to chance.

The residence before them held a Bach manuscript that had caused a stir in the music world half a century earlier. Its discovery elicited both passionate support and intense skepticism—the one from those with fond hopes for a new chapter in the established canon, the other from purists who suspected a forgery. By the time scholars and specialists finally concurred that it was genuine, the general public had galloped after other sensations. But with its value established, different parties got involved. The manuscript changed hands several times, with transactions that were legal and otherwise. It had for some time been an object of Josephine's affections.

Cumin returned the crib sheet to his coat pocket then pulled a newspaper from beneath his seat. He opened it to the local section and found the society notices. "I cannot fathom why these Americans feel compelled to broadcast their every action and intention so publicly," he said. "A cruise for this one, the engagement of another, this award, that recognition."

"It makes them feel connected, Mr. Cumin. After all, look at these homes." His arm swept across the gray vinyl dashboard, a finger aimed at the faux Tudor, Spanish Colonial and Craftsman mansions set on immaculate lawns up and down this street. "Don't they seem lonely?"

Hooded eyes peered at Trevor over the newspaper. "Lonely? I should say they are pathologically needy, having to display their wealth so blatantly. Loneliness is not their concern, but rather status." Cumin desperately needed a decent cup of tea, but tried to clear his mind of a desire with no prospect of fulfillment.

"The paper confirms it, Trevor," he said, resuming his professional voice. "Young Amanda Lionel of 21495 Rippling Brook Way will indeed be celebrating her enrollment to kindergarten. A grand party is being planned for August 12 by her proud parents, complete with pony rides, a bounce castle—whatever that may be—and a magician."

Cumin refolded the paper and set it on the van's floor. He lifted the padded top of the center console, withdrew a deck of cards and began shuffling them, first with his left hand, then with his right. "You mailed the flyers yesterday?" he asked.

Mouth full, Trevor nodded.

"And we know that even wealthy Americans cannot resist a bargain."

Trevor nodded again and then chased the scone with steaming coffee. He screwed the cap back on the thermos and wiped his mouth with the back of his hand. "Particularly when the magician they've depended on has a terrible accident that requires an extended stay in hospital, and they need a replacement on short notice."

The Bell Tower occupied prime real estate in a city that had briefly been the nation's capital, and like other institutions of its kind, the Bell, as it was known, exuded history in a sublime, dignified manner from each clay-fired brick. Its outer glass doors were flanked by evergreens and guarded by rotating shifts of stocky men who polished the brass handles vigorously and often. Inside, the lobby floors of marble from Pietrasanta, a quarry on the slopes of Monte Altissima in central Italy, gleamed. Matching dry sinks of burled mahogany topped with more marble sat against opposite walls; on each stood vases bursting with fresh flowers that were changed daily. A multilingual staff sat or stood behind a teak reception desk around the clock.

Prominent for its size when first built, the Bell was now dwarfed by clusters of skyscrapers. But its restricted height, by way of comparison, gave it the cachet of history. Inside, plaques affixed to understated wallpaper emphasized that pedigree. According to reliably documented tradition, Ben Franklin had domiciled in this establishment for some months, and the traveling evangelist George Whitefield had kept rooms, as well.

The Bell had aged gracefully, and its apartments stayed full, occupied by tenants who appreciated history while expecting every modern convenience. That required a steady stream of artisans, builders and mechanics capable of installing requisite updates while complying with conventional standards of preservation. Thankfully, the Bell's competent staff managed with efficiency and discretion the flow of workers and salespeople that filed into her lobby each day.

Max liked the place as soon as he stepped inside. He ran a finger over rich wood surfaces, inhaled deeply from a bouquet of white roses, let his shoes sink into the dense Persian rug where a pair of brocaded wingback chairs invited conversation. He waited while the concierge dealt with a rotund painter and then sauntered to the reception desk.

"I'm here to see Wilma Ritter," he told the man behind the counter.

The Bell's day manager peered over his pince-nez. "Whom shall I say is calling?"

"Richard Starkey," Max said. "Esquire." He grinned.

The clerk scowled at Max, then picked up a phone and punched numbers into its keypad. "A gentleman in the lobby is asking for you, Ms. Ritter. A Mr. Richard Starkey. Do you wish me to send him up?" He paused. "Very well."

The manager cradled the phone then spoke to Max. "Ms. Ritter is in the penthouse on eight, so you will need my key."

Max held out a hand, which evoked the manager's disdain. "I shall accompany you." He nodded to the attractive brunette seated behind him, who rose silently and slid into the space vacated as the manager came around to join Max. "Through here," he said, walking away from Max and turning the corner next to a full length mirror.

The elevator door was open when Max caught up; the manager stood inside, his key in the panel that had buttons running only to seven. "Our penthouse once had the city's most magnificent view," he said as the compartment closed soundlessly. "From its windows one may still glimpse the river."

"Nice sunsets, too, I bet, given the smog," said Max.

Beside him, the manager winced.

Uncle Sty had arranged this visit. Once Max had told him that a Babe Ruth card owner lived downtown, Bedford dialed into his network and found a contact who could make introductions. He then called Wilma Ritter, outlined the imminent threat and promised to send someone who could help. The lift stopped with a gentle bounce and as the door glided open, Max stepped out.

"Ms. Ritter will send you down once your business is concluded." With that, the elevator shuttered closed and Max was standing on patterned mauve carpet in a wainscoted vestibule. Its chandelier burned despite a large window behind him that filled the space with sunlight.

A woman was leaning against the jamb of an open door at the far end of the foyer. "Ringo," she said. "How good of you to drop by."

She was eighty, sixty, a hundred and ten. Max couldn't tell. Short, rake handle slim with gray hair cut close, she had silver hoops big enough for frisbee golf dangling from her ears. Toned arms showed the brown spots of sun and age. Dancing sky blue eyes saw through him into tomorrow.

A cigarette pinched into a holder clamped by her teeth glowed behind half an inch of ash. It didn't move as she spoke. "Well don't just stand there. Get in here, boy, and tell me what sort of game you've got in mind."

After the black Jaguar ahead of them slid into a parking space, Trevor steered the silver minivan to another spot close by. Cumin was consulting his watch.

"This shopping center is three miles from the Grassleby estate?"

Trevor checked the GPS suctioned to the van's windscreen. "Aye."

"We shall also need time and distance between this and our next target," Cumin said. "Do you have the flash drive?"

Trevor patted his shirt pocket.

"And the diagnostic tool?"

"Yes, Mr. Cumin." He laid the small device on the console's padded surface and reached back for another scone. "Have you changed your mind, Mr.

Cumin?" he asked, hopeful that his employer would enjoy a snack with him.

The older man scowled. Instead he pulled a plastic bottle of spring water from the door's cup holder and unscrewed the top. Before taking a drink, Cumin swiveled in his seat, to look again at the bags neatly arranged in the third row behind him. The fruit of their labors thus far, after stopovers in Singapore, New Zealand and Guatemala.

Amazing, Cumin reflected, on how careful packing of one's suitcases could both protect and conceal valuables. He took additional precautions, of course: he always dressed fashionably but not ostentatiously when traveling, he was unfailingly deferential to customs officials and he used the multiple passports in his possession according to a strict schedule. On occasions when he and Trevor worked together, he also required that they travel independently.

The slender, gracefully aging man was proud of his success. Moreover, he had never been to prison, had never been seriously considered as a suspect; to the best of his knowledge, only a very few would have even seen him to be a threat. Such status was nearly unprecedented in his chosen line of work. Cumin had sized his ego to his aspirations, and since he hoped for a long life in a place of his own choosing, the former had shrunk considerably. On occasion, he might have wished for more recognition of his prowess, but in deference to a future of freedom, he embraced a present of anonymity.

Now Cumin viewed the bags of Josephine's treasures with quiet pride. In a matter of weeks, they would be rid of this place and back home in Europe, having satisfied Josephine's latest whims. Even if his dove should not praise him overtly (and Cumin knew this was likely), it was enough that he had accomplished what gave her such pleasure. He would deliver what she had ordered and then retire to his modest flat in Greece for a well-deserved holiday, there to await his mistress's next bidding.

The van's engine fired, startling Cumin.

"The space across from the Jaguar is vacant," Trevor explained.

"Very well."

Trevor sped through the lot, ducking into a slot another had also noticed. This driver, a tiny woman in a forest green Humvee, screamed at him in her hermetically sealed vehicle. He favored her with a high wattage smile. Once parked, Trevor left the accessories switched on so that Mr. Cumin could listen to the radio if he so pleased. Then he opened the drawer beneath his seat and extracted an ice pick.

"I'll return in a moment," he said to Mr. Cumin, who was staring out his window, rolling a quarter over the knuckles of his left hand simply by flexing his attenuated fingers. Cumin turned to Trevor, nodded, and made the quarter disappear. He opened both hands, palms down, closed them both simultaneously, and then the quarter spurted out again, this time to dance along the ridges of his right hand.

"That's one of my favorite tricks," Trevor said before gently closing the door.

He was back almost before Cumin registered his absence. Both men sat quietly in the van, Cumin splaying and then curling his fingers into balls, Trevor reading a paperback and eating scones.

The lights on the Jaguar in front of them flashed; the car gave a muted beep. A smartly dressed woman laden with the results of her shopping was approaching the car, keys held by a hand that also tried to keep a bright red bag from falling to the pavement. She reached the sedan, opened the trunk and filled it with her packages.

After slamming the lid, she walked around to the driver's door, where she spotted the flat front tire. Both hands went to her hips, she turned full circle and laughed. She punched the key fob again and once more the trunk clicked open. Restraining clips pinned a jack to the side of the trunk; she pulled it clear. When she lowered the trunk's lid a second time, Trevor was standing next to the car, worry on his face.

"In for a spot of trouble, it appears," he said. "Might I be of assistance?"

"How gallant of you," the woman replied. "But I am quite capable of changing a tire."

"No doubt," Trevor said. "But all the same, I should be pleased to help."

The sleeves of his plaid shirt were rolled to the elbow, his jeans were neatly pressed, it was full daylight in a crowded place—this man, despite his size, was no threat to her.

"In that case, yes, thanks. I'd welcome it."

Trevor held out a hand for the jack, even though he looked fit enough to lift the vehicle without its aid. Once it was wedged in place, he turned the crank, raising the car until the injured tire barely touched the tarmac. Then he loosened the lug nuts and returned to the jack. When the tire was completely in the air, he pulled off the nuts, removed the tire and let it clatter to the ground.

"I'll just fetch the spare," he said to the watching woman.

Noticing his perspiration, she asked "Can I offer you a drink?"

Trevor smiled. "Perhaps when I finish."

She pressed him. "What would you like?"

The bulky man stood upright. "I've developed a taste for the root beer you Yanks have. Nothing like it back home."

The woman hesitated. She would have preferred to give him a water bottle from the trunk. But he had been so kind. "There's a service station just over there," she said. "Let me see if they have root beer."

"Please," Trevor said. "Don't go to any bother. I'll have this finished in a tick, and then be on my way."

"It's no bother," she said. "I'll be right back." Without further argument, she headed for the station, checking her purse surreptitiously to make sure she still had the Jaguar's keys.

Trevor watched her walk away as he set the spare in place and tightened the lug nuts by hand. Then he opened the driver's door. First he leaned over to open the glove box, where he found a recent receipt for routine service. The name on the bill matched the logo embossed on the sedan's rear license plate holder. Next, Trevor tugged at a cluster of wires under the steering column, dislodging the computer receptacle.

A metallic rectangle with a trailing cable came out of Trevor's back pocket; he inserted a flash drive into its port and jacked into the Jaguar's diagnostic plug.

Trevor pressed a switch on his device. Its green light blinked once and then stayed on. He looked back toward the service station and saw no sign of the woman. The light turned red and he broke the connection, then carefully tucked the wire yoke back in place. The large man, both deft and agile, slid out of the car and was tightening the new wheel's nuts with a crossbar when the woman returned. She held a large plastic cup in one hand.

"All the root beer you could possibly want in one day," she said, offering him the drink. He grinned, rose and wiped a hand across his brow. Then he accepted the cup and took a long pull from the straw.

"Marvelous," he said. "My very great thanks."

"So then, is all well with the old girl?" the woman asked, patting the Jaguar's fender.

"She's good as new," Trevor said. Then he pointed to the trunk. "Would you mind opening the boot?"

"Of course." She pressed the key fob to raise the trunk's lid.

Trevor secured the damaged tire then shut the trunk. He collected his root beer from the pavement and raised it in a salute. "Have a nice day," he said, and then sauntered off.

He walked until the Jaguar had pulled out of its spot and driven away, then circled back to Cumin and the minivan.

"A splendid vehicle, the XJ8," Trevor said.

"Indeed," Cumin replied. "But susceptible to electrical failures, nonetheless."

Trevor nodded. "Trouble ahead for this one, eh?"

"Without doubt." The older man polished his watch's gold back with a thumb. "Provided Malcolm is up to his usual standards, in two weeks, this one will have developed the most annoying problems."

Trevor pulled out of the parking spot, taking care not to crease the car next to him. "But nothing the English Motors Group can't repair."

"You've confirmed that they do indeed offer pick up and drop off service to their clientele?" Cumin replaced the watch in his vest pocket.

"Aye."

"Now I wonder," Cumin said. "Do you suppose we're likely to find an individual among the EMG who might be amenable to the offer of a day's paid vacation, in exchange for permitting you to deliver the vehicle once it has been repaired?"

Calloused fingers curled around the minivan's leather-wrapped steering wheel. "I've discovered a pub where a fair few of those boys go for a pint after work," Trevor said. "They've Guinness on tap, as well, Mr. Cumin, in case you'd be interested."

11

Wilma Ritter did not suffer fools gladly, and so dialog with Max was a delight. Stuyvesant Bedford, the man who had contacted her regarding a possible threat to her personal belongings, had promised she would find the young man he was sending to be charming; she was pleased that he had been correct. As Max fleshed out the details of what she had learned during that initial conversation with Mr. Bedford, Wilma became more animated.

"Hell's bells, boy. If this English fella thinks he can sidle into my place and stroll off with the Babe, he's gonna have to negotiate with Mr. Smith—" she took a long drag from the cigarette.

"Mr. Smith?" Max asked. "I thought you were a widow."

"Never married," she corrected him. "And you didn't let me finish, boy. That's Mr. Smith and Mr. Wesson. Taught many a body the important lessons in life, don't you know."

Max grinned. "No doubt. But I think, Ms. Ritter, that in this case, it's best we not tangle with international art thieves."

The woman snorted. "First off, young man, call me Wilma. And second, don't patronize me. I been slinging guns since afore you were in long pants. My idea of a nice quiet evening at home is to field strip a Glock 19."

"Four hundred channels and still nothing to watch?" Max asked.

The woman grunted from her armchair.

"OK, Wilma, I hear you, and I expect you'd just as soon stick around and pick these Brits off like beer cans. But there's also getting the stuff they're holding, and making sure they don't try to pull these stunts any longer. I just don't think shooting them is going to accomplish that."

"You'd be surprised what a good bullet wound can accomplish," Wilma muttered.

A crash in the back reaches of Wilma's apartment made Max jump.

"For a guy who wants to dance with crooks, you're pretty high strung, aren't you?" she said through clenched teeth. She removed the cigarette holder. "No cause for alarm. I got me a fella in here to repair leaks from the roof garden. Last rain storm, water ran in and ruined my ceiling and a piece of the wall. On account of this prehistoric construction, I had to hire somebody who knew his way around plaster and lath." The woman tapped ash into a pottery tray. "Course after that, it'll need paint and then there's an electrician since that wall connects with the kitchen. Water messed up my appliances something fierce. I ain't had a minute's peace to myself in this place for a month, and I'm not expectin' things to calm down for another two or three."

Perfect, Max thought, and then he tried to change the subject. "Let me ask you, Wilma, one collector to another, how did you come by a Ruth rookie card?"

Smoke clouded her face. Wilma reached for a glass from the table next to the chair where she sat. "Lottery," she said.

Max's eyebrows rose.

"Yep, I hit the big time, eight years ago last month. They say the lottery's a tax on stupidity, an' I'd probably agree. But stupid is as stupid does, whatever that means. I been buyin' me a ticket every day down the gas station next to the Dollar General. Same numbers each time, too, the phone number of my high school sweetheart. Every night, I'm watching TV, and cleaning my gun." She peered at Max through a wreath of smoke. "Then one night, it's my numbers there on the screen. Couple weeks later, I am one rich cracker."

"What happened after that?" Max asked, fascinated.

"Made me a whole boatload of new best friends is what. People I barely knew, and relatives I'd plum forgot showed up, asking for a piece of this, offering me advice on that. I listened for a while, then did what I pleased."

Max had no trouble imagining that.

"Went on a cruise, around the world. Finally saw the Taj Mahal. Do you know it's made of tile all the way up? Gives a body a headache just to look but, sakes alive, it is downright stupendous. When I got back, I found me an apartment, this one, in fact. Saw it in a magazine at the hairdressers and thought it might be nice to live in a city. And I bought me a Babe Ruth baseball card." She stubbed out the cigarette, set a fresh one in the holder and flicked a dime store lighter. Smoke curled toward the ceiling.

"Do you know I actually saw Ruth play? I was small, and he was in pinstripes, but I was there. Hit a home run that day, he did, as per usual. So I had this connection with the fella, and a lot of money to boot. Figured I'd invest in something people smarter 'n me thought was valuable."

"Can I see it?" Max asked.

"Sure," Wilma said. "He's down yonder." She waved to her left. "Help yourself."

Max rose and turned toward the hall. The card hung behind glass in a brushed metal frame, alone except for a rectangle of parchment with typed details regarding authentication. "You just keep it out in the open like this?" Max called back to her.

"You ever seen what a Glock 19 can do?" she called after him in a raspy voice. "And I don't get out much."

"Which brings me to my other point for visiting today, Wilma," Max said, returning to the room and taking his seat once more. "As best we can figure, this thief operates in broad daylight. Blends in with others who ought to be there, and before you know it, what he had his eye on is gone." Max was taking liberties here, pressing his theory. His uncle was not completely convinced, but had decided to let Max follow through on his idea. In the meantime, Bedford was moving a few of his own pieces around the board, preparing for the end game.

"He's coming to the Bell, Wilma," Max said, wanting to emphasize his point. "But I don't want him in your place."

"Very noble of you. But how you gonna take care of that?"

Max patted the mottled Spaniel that had ambled over to sit by his chair. "These workers for your apartment and others—the painters, electricians and so forth—they need to check in at the desk before they use the elevator, right?"

She nodded.

"What if you're not here?"

"Then the staff in the lobby would tell them to come back another time."

"Perfect."

"But I'm always here," she protested.

"Funny," Max said. "I thought you were going on another cruise."

She scowled. "You want me to leave just when things get exciting?"

"It's only a couple of weeks, til the smoke clears."

She drew in from the cigarette then exhaled in his direction.

"You know what I mean. Let me see if I can work with the folks downstairs, so they can steer our crook elsewhere when he tries to get into your place."

"And when do you figure that's likely to be?"

"I expect Mr. Bedford laid out his theory?" Max asked. "We're not totally sure, but he's betting on July seven, based on previous experience with this outfit."

"July seven, huh?" Wilma tossed a knotted rag in front of the Spaniel. The dog yawned. "Yeah, after your boss hung up, I got to thinking." She threw the dog a leather bone, but again no reaction. "You got a problem if this crook is supposed to be part of the crowd that's coming and going."

Max felt his stomach tighten. "Problem?"

Wilma left her seat to retrieve a slip of paper that rested on a desk behind her. "According to this, there's gonna be just over a week around July fourth without people tracking in dirt all over the carpets. Says here construction workers have a bunch of days off in honor of Independence Day and all. Some sort of union deal, I guess." She squinted at the page, reading the small print. Then she stared at Max. "So since the Bell's not having any outside traffic on the seventh anyhow, there's no need for me to skedaddle, I guess." She smiled in triumph, settled back in her chair and lit another cigarette.

Max was calculating rapidly in his head, trying to figure whether that weekend would require a change in Collingsworth's plans for the other owners. He'd have to discuss that with Sty. His idea could still work, but they would need to shift a few things in the timing. Speaking to Wilma, he said, "So he won't be here on the seventh, but that doesn't mean he'll cross you off his list. I still need you to plan a vacation, just one that starts a little later. Can I call you with the dates?"

She chuckled. "I still like my idea of lying in wait so's I can roll out blastin', but I guess I'm willing to play it your way. Although so far, to be honest, I'm not that impressed." Wilma puffed thoughtfully. "What did you say your line of work was again, Mr. Starkey?"

Max settled back in his chair. "My name is Max," he said. "And I find things."

"You any good at that?" she asked. "'Cause it sounds to me like you're behind in the count."

Max nodded toward the hallway. "So far, I've got a pretty good average." The Spaniel dozed on the floor beside him while Max absently scratched its ears. "This time, though, I'm swinging for the fences."

12

Unlike his nephew, Stuyvesant Bedford had finished college. His family had been skeptical about the need for or value of higher learning, but high school teachers had spotted promise and prodded. Sty enrolled in college despite comments from his uncles, wanting to set an example for his younger siblings, hoping he'd find a major that held his interest. He thought that would be Phys Ed, so he could coach, but then a required class in history grabbed him by the brain.

He discovered he liked French, too. It took six years, what with having to work on the farm summers and falls on account of his deadbeat father, but he finally finished. By then he'd had his fill of rural America and was ready for adventure. He'd stopped by an Army recruiter's table during a college job fair on a dare—Viet Nam was winding down, and the military seemed irrelevant—only to get sucked into the vortex of the recruiter's enthusiasm.

Six weeks later, Bedford was on a bus, bound for the Army's officer basic course. Scores on tests there threw him into the intel pool with other young officers. More training, then a posting in Europe, to read, listen, chat up likely candidates for important data. Like his peers, Sty had a broad remit in the intelligence community, but also like them, he gravitated toward particular arenas. Of special interest was locating treasures that had gone missing from various nations and returning them to their rightful owners. Sty liked being a positive force for history.

Along the way, Sty demonstrated a knack for developing fruitful contacts. One was Dulcinea. Being from the Philippines and blessed with a wide skill set, she easily moved around Asia, Africa and Europe without attracting any attention.

Another was Foxe, the Brit. The survivor of public school and a wayward youth, Foxe had made friends with villains and curators and others in between who were connected with the art world so that he could facilitate complex transfers and broker ransom negotiations. Foxe could write respected reviews of gallery shows or provide the phone numbers of parties with access to a lost Matisse or Manet. He also had a private collection many would have envied had they known of its existence. The compact, wiry man moonlighted as a fence on the continent as well, keeping an apartment in Montmartre and using a guise he'd perfected with long practice: thin mustache, ropy arms, volatile temper, easy laugh. He wore a black beret and dabbled as a landscape painter. His accent was perfect.

In the nineties, after the Wall was demolished, Sty Bedford had been temporarily at a loss. With borders relaxed and people flowing freely between countries, much of the information he'd once had to beg, borrow and steal was now easy to procure, or of little current worth. Sty faced his options dispassionately: he'd done his twenty plus a couple, so a modest pension was set. That, along with an account in the Caymans he'd been feeding surreptitiously, gave financial security, but he was too young to check out and play golf. The thought of sitting at bars, trading on past glories, galled him even more. Sty bought a round-the-world ticket instead. For him, life gained clarity at forty thousand feet.

Shifts in governments weren't new, although this latest upheaval was far bigger than the typical third world coup. All that change left a body scrambling for alliances, and wondering whose side you were on, and who your enemy was this week. Sty enjoyed adventure as much as the next guy, but at this point in his life, he was ready for a few grams of stability.

He wrote on seat back tray tables, with a plastic cup of mediocre coffee on one corner and his elbow jostled by passengers in the middle seats. The steppes of China, deserts of Australia and roiling seas off Cape Horn passed below while he filled a fat spiral notebook with ideas and observations. Intelligence work was all he cared about, but paradoxically, politics annoyed him. Finally a way out of the dilemma occurred to him during a trek through the rugged Torres del Paine in Chile's southern cone. There at the bottom of the earth, an idea as simple as all great discoveries occurred to him: he'd switch to art fulltime.

Studying history in college had introduced him to a world he'd never dreamed about given a family with no time for oil paintings or bas relief. Subsequent classes while in uniform honed his interest and expertise. A series of postings in Europe combined with frequent travel gave him access to the world's great museums;

he would wander for hours in the Louvre, the Tate, the Prado, the Rijksmuseum, fascinated by what hung on the walls or stood on a dais.

His work also gave him access to treasures less well-known but every bit as interesting, since much of his day job had him chasing criminals who used art as an investment for their ill-gotten gains, or as a way of washing cash, or simply to add the fragrance of respectability to an otherwise putrid life. Having a van Gogh or Klee on hand also provided a good bargaining chip in the event one was apprehended by the authorities; these clandestine masterpieces made excellent 'get out of jail free' cards. When word of such pieces hit his desk, Sty would make sure to be in the vicinity when the doors got kicked in, or he'd ask for glossies of what his buddies recovered at a drug lord's castle or a banking executive's yacht.

Sty's global circumnavigation ended in London. He deplaned at Heathrow, found a phone and dialed the Sullivan Corporation in DC, to talk about a standing job offer. Bedford had met Bart Sullivan while on assignment in Cairo; the two had discussed Britain's fascination with the antiquities of other nations. Their paths crossed after that and in between, Sully bugged Sty about joining his company.

"It's a private firm with government contracts," Sullivan had once told him over espresso at a Paris café. "Basically we're information brokers, but we also like field ops. That's where I'd see you doing well, Bedford. We handle a lot of recovery work—high end, sensitive stuff that doesn't move well through official channels. An art guy like you, with your experience? Perfect fit."

Shortly after the call, Bedford left government service for a corner office at the private firm. Sully had been right: he was a natural when it came to art recovery. It helped that he liked the stuff, had a nose for what was authentic and what was some Caravaggio wanna-be's best effort. Not only that, but in this new job, Sty didn't have to factor in a political agenda. He concentrated on the paintings, sculptures, jewelry and friezes that needed retrieving; deeper questions he left to the philosophers.

Some of the people he ran into as a brain for hire were familiar, like Josephine. His first exposure to this most peculiar of collectors had been near the end of his freshman tour with the Army. She was a newbie with a thin file, more annoying than dangerous. That meant the young lieutenant had drawn the short straw when it came to finding her lair and flushing her out. He tried to take the duty seriously, but Phine's case was one of several in his portfolio, and never rose to priority status. When another assignment sent him to the Caribbean near what he'd figured was her current nest, he'd swooped in for a quick and easy score, reasoning that any arrest would help with a promotion.

That was the night she threw him the Venetian pencil holder and got under his skin. Josephine had walked away unscathed, but his failure made the rounds. He'd covered the damage with other successes, the way an artist painted over an inferior scene with fresh oils and a better vision. Meanwhile, the troublesome woman dropped off his radar and none of the higher ups demanded pursuit. Sty's arrest rate improved, and he got those promotions.

During that second encounter, at her villa in Monaco, he'd nearly died. Once again, he'd been working a different case but, because he never fully let her go, Sty's ears perked up when he caught wind of activity with Phine at the center. Using a tip coughed up by one of his sources, Sty had found the villa. He cornered Josephine on a balcony and was about to put the cuffs on when a quartet of Italians burst in, guns blazing. Apparently this time she'd stolen from a residence in Milan whose owner took her intrusion as a personal insult. She scooted through a side door; he got caught in the crossfire. Josephine went to ground after that, except for making a quick visit to Sty during his recuperation. She'd left a sketch next to his hospital bed while he was sleeping. Her note claimed it was a Rembrandt.

Sty found her third party, in Rio, a day late. This time, the apartment she had used was a pile of rubble. From that, Sty surmised that one of her targets had a very short fuse, and that Josephine was finally out of business for good. He closed the file and got busy with other responsibilities; when he left the Army for the private sector, she was just part of the back story for the scars on his chest.

He enjoyed Sullivan's shop. One spring shortly after he joined the firm, reports crossed his desk regarding a spike in activity on the art world's shadow side. Later that fall, it was quiet again, and Sty forgot the earlier chatter. Then a few years later, Sty got an invitation in the mail, to a birthday party in late July, in Cabo san Lucas, on Mexico's Baja peninsula. It was signed "J."

Pressing business in Germany kept Sty from attending, but the note was enough to reopen a dormant file. He didn't expect much, and was plenty busy elsewhere, but Josephine still warranted an occasional glance. As had been the case before, however, she kept a low profile, and what she managed to abscond with hardly ruffled significant feathers. Once more she slipped far back in Sty's queue of important concerns. It wasn't until he'd settled in Montana that Josephine mattered again.

She was making mincemeat of his new firm's accounts. Clients paid handsomely to protect their goods; admittedly, they wanted protection of items for which they had questionable claim, but that detail aside, it was still a matter of offering a reliable service. If Sty's colleagues couldn't keep things where they were meant to stay, or failed to find what had walked off, the business would crater, soon and loudly.

That was unacceptable to Sty, who liked this new company. Guiding tourists so they could bag a moose or photograph bighorn sheep was all well and good, but next to recovering a Cézanne oil or returning an Aztec mask, there was no comparison. He fully intended to keep his job, and refused to let Phine alter those plans. So he reached out to Dulcinea and Foxe, with positive results.

He hired Max, too, because he liked the kid and saw potential. But there were still gaps. That, and he needed new blood, rather than an old standby. Sty consulted his mental list of prospects, until one face came into focus. A former colleague, someone who had trained Sty in his early days, but then had departed the hallowed halls of intrigue. At the time, Sty had put that down to weakness, but staying in touch with his former mentor had shown Sty that sometimes people change. Getting out had helped his friend move into a different sort of life.

The guy hadn't gone completely soft, either. When his daughter got bit by the adventure bug, he had contacted Sty through some of their dusty back channels, asking if Bedford might have a suitable gig. Up until now there hadn't been any need, so Sty had just filed the information for another time. But, he remembered her father saying she was fluent in Spanish, Portuguese and Italian. A cool head, too, he had said. And dependable, especially for a person her age. About the same age, Sty reflected, as his nephew.

This time, Sty was determined to nab Josephine. He dug into his hard drive, to make sure the patterns he thought he'd detected weren't just the product of an overactive imagination. But the dates checked out and now, having the benefit of hindsight along with much more data, he could see that every seven years Josephine threw a big party in late July when she gave out favors. Everything compact, and nothing, as far as Sty could tell, that ever edged above half a mill. That was a sizeable amount for some households but, in the grand scheme, it wasn't high enough to trip alarms.

Ingenious, Sty had to admit, but still weird. Go to all that work and then give stuff away? That, or just wire the place with explosives and blow it all to smithereens. Either way, some odd habits on display by this woman.

In addition to what had been taken, Bedford's lists also gave dates of activity—activity which, he had noticed, definitely increased past typical in the run-up to Phine's seventh-year party. Apparently she was contracting an assortment of thieves for her shopping spree. One other detail was finally obvious once he looked closely at the 'when' list: things got hopping in February, March, May, July and November, and during these months, on dates that were prime numbers.

You're kidding me, Sty had thought when he noticed that pattern. But then he paused, recalling that most crooks, like most people, had a method to their madness. Josephine seemed to be captivated by primes, those unique and strange digits scattered along the number line. He speculated that she thought of herself in similar terms.

Fair enough. If Sty's theory was correct, then Collingsworth was using June to lay groundwork, preparing for his blitz in July. But which of the prime-numbered dates in that month would he choose? Bedford stared at the columns he'd fashioned after collating data on the various heists. He'd further refined his information by creating rows, separating each 'party year' from the others with a heavy blue line.

There had been six of these, Sty noticed, with a seventh evidently underway. Seven parties, another prime, with seven years between parties. Sty was excited now, tapping the pencil on the desk until the tip broke off. Phine's birthday was at the end of July—the thirty-first, itself a prime. The irresistible symmetry drew Sty to conclude that Collingsworth would marshal his efforts to strike on the seventh of July. He'd relayed that to Max, certain of his calculations.

Foxe's tip about de Groot and the photographs had told him what and where. The paper in front of him established when. He'd sent Max in to lay the traps and from two thousand miles away, Sty watched the noose close.

Not long, now.

13

The baseball card troubled Cumin. In all his years working for Josephine, he had never questioned her methods or her taste. The former were peculiar, but then, adopting a career as a thief was itself peculiar, so who was he to judge? As to her taste, Cumin had had occasion to observe it at close range, and he found Josephine's style and sensibilities to be exquisite. Not only had he stolen much of what she liked to give to others at her birthday parties, but there was also the array of objects she had kept for herself. A few of these had appeared on account of Cumin's industry, but the rest she had acquired by purchase, shrewd trading, or through another's agency.

This last point gave Cumin cause for regret. He wondered, on occasion, why he alone had not been deemed worthy of securing everything she wanted. Had he not demonstrated by now his fealty to Josephine? Was there any bridge he would not cross? Any mountain he would not climb? Yet she persisted in hiring others.

She had told him it was merely business. Diversification is a sound principle in any line of work, she had said. But he suspected then, as he suspected now, ulterior motives. She was an inveterate shopper—who knew this better than he?—and so he supposed she was in the market for another to usurp him, using contracts to audition potential replacements.

All the more reason to prove himself indispensible, to hunt and gather so that all her wishes would be fulfilled. She would take him back—of this Cumin was certain—and while he might grovel, he would not whine. Best then to make sure the present wish list became a reality.

But the baseball card was, by any measure, odd. To his knowledge, Josephine had never indicated any interest in sport. And this particular specimen: Cumin fingered the picture they had made from the flash drive sent over by the Frenchman. It was ordinary, pedestrian. In a word, vulgar. Printed on cardboard, featuring a grinning man holding a fat stick of wood: who could possibly take this seriously?

Cumin knew that some had, that certain influential people in their infinite wisdom had assigned to this card a value far surpassing many of the gems and paintings Cumin routinely liberated so as to pay his own bills. Items such as these had been valued for centuries, but lately, a medley of strange objects with no pedigree had been fetching astronomical prices at auction. This only fed the mania. Results at Sotheby's or Christie's or any one of a dozen reputable houses established worth these days, and historical value was becoming a thing of the past. Cumin did not like this development. At the same time, his chosen profession required an awareness of trends.

A card like the one Josephine had requested was rare. At present it vied with a small handful of others to be the most valuable of its class, but even if it never achieved supremacy, the card had managed to maintain a consistent market value in excess of a quarter million dollars. That was a number Cumin could understand, one that fit comfortably in the range of value for what Josephine liked to give away at her celebrations. That is, if she didn't on some whim decide that for this particular party she was going to set explosives, hurry guests outside and arrange for a spectacular night of fireworks. Cumin laid that thought aside. He might be a thief but he was no cretin.

Josephine had in her day destroyed some irreplaceable works of art, and Cumin felt a twinge of guilt for his complicity. Yes, he had a modicum of sorrow that extraordinary pieces—art he had at one time carried with his own hands—had now gone extinct, but devotion to Josephine prohibited recrimination. He did what needed to be done.

This card, however, was not art. Cumin thought to ask Josephine about her intentions regarding it, but quickly quashed that impulse. She has her reasons, he told himself, and that will suffice. Still, it was a problem he mulled on occasion, when the waiting grew tedious.

He was pondering the question now, as he and Trevor sat at an outdoor table in the very heart of Philadelphia. Trevor had ordered another of his coffee monstrosities. Cumin had risked tea, because this establishment looked like it might have staff up to the task. But he had been disappointed, just as he was disappointed with the pastry that accompanied it. Trevor, on the other hand, was ecstatic with his food. Once again he had discovered something about America that evoked delight: macaroni and cheese covered by a crust of charred bread crumbs.

"Do you intend to eat that?" Cumin asked, as the server set a brimming tureen in front of Trevor.

"Indeed I do, Mr. Cumin." He bent over the bowl and inhaled. "All this driving has made me ravenous. Would you care for a sample?"

It took all Cumin's willpower not to gag.

Trevor attacked his pasta with vigor and Cumin thought he meant to lick the dish clean. He interrupted what would most certainly have been an uncomfortable scene with a question.

"Have you noticed how many workmen are in and out of that apartment?"

"I have; it's been quite a parade," Trevor said.

"Agree—" said Cumin. Then a jolt went through the thin man. "Did you say parade?"

Trevor nodded, his mouth full of baguette.

"The gods are conspiring," Cumin muttered. "How could I have been so stupid?"

"No."

Max didn't like to contradict his uncle, who had been around the block several times before Max could even walk, but in this case, he was sure Sty's idea about July seven was wrong. Collingsworth would not try to hit all three on the same day, and the seventh of July would not be his intended date, either. Max was confident about his own theory, namely that the thief operated in broad daylight, and needed people to be around when he struck.

Closure on the seventh would render the Bell unassailable. Max reckoned that the other homes their opponents were watching would be shut tight for the long holiday weekend, as well. Collingsworth would appear on another day. Other days, Max corrected himself. He won't try three at once. He can't.

Uncle Sty had listened, protested, and then reluctantly agreed with Max's conclusions. The only question then was which of the remaining days in July Collingsworth would use. With Phine's birthday on the thirty-first, Collingsworth needed to be done by then, but that still left the eleventh, thirteenth, seventeenth, nineteenth, and the twenty-third. The twenty-ninth, too, if Collingsworth decided to cut it close and hop a red-eye back to Europe.

Too many options, Sty thought, trying not to worry that he'd overlooked the obvious, or that his nephew might be barking up the wrong tree. Thinking more data might narrow the scope, Sty called Dulcinea after talking with Max, asking that her niece sniff around for clues. Then he rang Foxe, who didn't pick up. Sty left a message.

Max needed details before he went back to Wilma concerning her imminent vacation, so while he waited for Sty to unearth information, he drove to Orange's place, to ask about borrowing his card.

Orange didn't answer when Max knocked on the door; a peek inside the garage confirmed that he was not at home. Max debated forcing his way inside, but thought better of that option. An hour passed, and then much of a second, and Max had decided to return another time when Orange's ominous black cruiser turned on to his block and made for the house. Max got out of his car and waited for the cop to park.

"Hey, Orange," Max said, walking up to the cruiser.

"Hi, Max," the other returned. He was leaning against the car's fender. "And by the way, I go by Fire these days."

Max nodded. "I heard. But it doesn't suit you. Besides, I only ever knew you as Orange."

The solid young man smiled. "Yeah, that was a good name. Way better than Byron."

Max laughed. "I figured you'd appreciate a different handle. You never would have made it out of high school otherwise."

"You were right," Fire agreed. "But once I put on this uniform, I needed a more professional—"

" 'Fire' sounds professional?" Max asked.

"More than Orange." Hands went into his pockets. "Did you come over for something in particular?"

Max shuffled his feet. Now it was his turn to be self-conscious. "I did. Two things, actually. First, I need the card." Max didn't specify; between the two of them, the memento of Babe Ruth's rookie year had always and only been 'the card'.

"Should I be knowing why?" Fire asked.

"If I told you," Max said, "that badge might force you to do something that in the short and long run wouldn't be very helpful."

"Is that a fact?" Fire weighed his options. What would Roma do in this situation? Obvious: she would trust Max, no matter what.

"And the second?"

Max stared at the man who had been his friend in high school, the kid who had been at his side nearly every day since they had learned to read. A memory floated into Max's mind: two boys, running through a vacant lot toward bicycles as, behind them, a tree stump disintegrated with a dramatic flash and a satisfying boom. Orange turning to Max, amazed at what they'd done; Max pleased by the results of his experiment with black powder. Now Orange was a cop.

Max crossed his arms, inspected the driveway, let his hands fall to his sides. "Orange," he said. "Well, I guess I've been nursing this grudge a long time, but I'm the one getting sick. I got to thinking about the way we were friends, and how much that meant. And that I—" The speech Max had rehearsed in his mind on the drive over was unraveling. He would start blubbering in a minute and he wasn't about to go that far. Max took a breath and spoke in a level voice. "Anyway, what I wanted was to say I'm sorry."

"It's about time," Fire said with a stern face.

Max stared at Orange, preparing a protest.

"Of course I forgive you," Fire said, breaking into a lopsided grin.

"Great." Max calmed, cleared his throat. Realized his good fortune. "Now, can we talk about the card?"

"Sure." Fire picked up the oversized lunch pail at his feet and headed for the house. "So long as we can also talk about Roma."

14

Trevor was concerned with his employer's mood swings and pessimism. Despite a notable string of successes in his field and the muted though widespread admiration of his peers, Mr. Cumin lacked confidence. I need to cheer him up, Trevor thought.

The burly man set the baguette he had been consuming on the plate in front of him. "Come now, Mr. Cumin," he said. "What seems to be the trouble?"

Cumin's head was between hands that kneaded his temples. He spoke without looking up. "These bloody Yanks," he muttered.

Trevor was still at a loss. Unblinking eyes met his as Cumin moaned. "Independence Day, Trevor. July the fourth. The day these infernal colonies broke away from the Crown."

"July four, did you say, Mr. Cumin?"

"Indeed. I had hoped we might conclude our business within the month's first week, but as the fourth falls on a weekend this year, we're certain to lose at least three days that might otherwise have been of value. How could I have forgotten?" Again, his head slumped. "No doubt those other households in which we are interested will be away at the mountain cabin or beach condominium, as well."

"Mr. Cumin." Trevor tried not to sound patronizing. This man was renowned for his skills and composure. He also paid very well. "We still have several other acceptable days in the month on which to carry out our assignments, do we not?"

When Cumin did not answer, Trevor tried another tack. "I've no doubt that you will devise a way to fulfill our contract so that she—Trevor never named Miss Wainwright in public—will have reason to rejoice."

This roused the other man. "Perhaps you're right," he said. Cumin turned the tea cup's handle to three o'clock and brushed a crumb from the table. Then he straightened the striped tie inside his cardigan. His professional demeanor had returned.

"I suppose we might improvise, once we ascertain when the workmen are likely to resume their labors," Cumin said, gesturing toward the Bell.

"A problem easily solved," Trevor said, rising from the redwood chair. He crossed the street and with a nod to the liveried doorman, entered the apartment building. Half a cup of dreadful tea later, Cumin saw him exit from the same door to return to their table. Trevor opened the embossed folder he carried, extracting a scrap of paper.

"'Residents should know that during the period of July two to seven, all construction work in the Bell Tower will be temporarily suspended in recognition of our nation's birthday celebration'," he read.

Cumin examined his companion with surprise.

"I asked for information about available housing units, and while the clerk at the desk was preparing a packet of information, I noticed this leaflet on the counter," Trevor said. "From what it says here, we can return with impunity any time after the seventh. Surely by then, following this extended holiday, the Bell Tower will be aflutter with activity."

"I'm impressed, Trevor," Cumin said.

"Your humble servant," the other man replied, without a hint of irony.

Bedford's phone chirped with an incoming text, the message from Foxe he'd been wanting. With a quick scan of the tiny screen, Sty had the information he needed. He called Max.

"Collingsworth is in line for one more job before the party," Sty told his nephew. "In Zurich. Apparently he'll get the call later today."

Max reviewed his European geography. "If he's trying to deliver goods to Portugal, he'll finish business here before he goes to Switzerland, right?"

Sty was nodding at his end. "Most likely. Makes sense he'll finish in the States as soon as possible, then fly over to Zurich so he can complete his work by the end of the month."

"That gives us our timetable, within a few days more or less," said Max.

"Yeah, but let's not forget we still have another problem," Sty said.

"Namely?"

"We not only have to stop Collingsworth and grab what he has, but we also need to figure a way into Phine's place and make off with the lot before the party takes place. I told you she's not above blowing it all to kingdom come, didn't I?"

Max enlarged the calendar on his computer screen. "First things first," he said. "Let's try to suss out this Limey's next moves and then we can worry about Ms. Wainwright."

"Listen, kid," Sty said. "About all I've been doing is worrying about that broad. But I'm with you on trying to figure when he'll hit us."

"That shouldn't be tough," Max said. "He needs to case the joint in Zurich, so he'll need to finish here as soon as possible. But the July fourth weekend must have messed up his plans a little."

"Yeah," said Sty. "That makes the eleventh and thirteenth our best bets. Maybe the seventeenth, too."

"Can he wait that long?" Max asked. "Would he leave that much time between jobs?"

His uncle was quiet before answering, working out Collingsworth's steps. Then he gave Max his conclusions. "If you're right that our guy won't try all three scores in one day, then we're probably looking for two days close together. That way there's less time for owners to discover the losses. My money's on July eleven and thirteen."

"So if we want to box him in, I'll need him at Wilma's late in the afternoon on one of those days."

"You got it, kid."

The phone rang at the Grassleby mansion, but no one heard it over the barking dog, blaring stereo and small children screaming for peanut butter without jelly unless it's marshmallow. Anything short of an air raid siren would have gone unnoticed. But in a brief lull—the dog found a shoe, the kids had full mouths, TV news broke for a commercial and the disc was changing in the player—one ring slipped through. Sunny Grassleby lunged for the cordless and squeezed it between her cheek and chin.

"Yes?" she said, stifling a laugh at the dog's determination with her husband's loafer. She snapped her fingers at the kids bent over their morning cereal, urging them to look at Mutters. Then she turned her attention to the caller. "I'm sorry, I missed that. What did you say?"

A voice on the other end was poor competition for the bedlam around her.

"Hang on," she said. "Let me put you on speaker." She laid the receiver on the counter, then hit a button on the base unit and another on the stereo's remote. With a frantic wave of her hand, she tried to silence the children. Mutters, the dog, had scurried off into another room to shred leather.

The other voice boomed. "Mrs. Grassleby? This is English Motors Group, about your Jaguar. I believe you rang us about a problem you were experiencing?"

"Oh, right," Sunny said, trying not to giggle as her daughter gargled grape juice.

"What seems to be the difficulty?"

"I have no idea. My husband wanted me to call you." Her husband, the big shot lobbyist, who figured you could fix any problem with a phone. "Part of your warranty, or something like that?"

"Precisely. In addition to the manufacturer's guarantees, English Motors Group stands behind every vehicle it sells. Can you bring the car in for our technicians to inspect?"

"Not really. You see, right now it's dead in our garage. I tried to use it yesterday but she just wouldn't start. Tiffany, get down from there right now!"

"Excuse me?"

"Sorry, I was just speaking to my daughter. There's a large brown spot under the front and she won't start at all."

"I see." The voice on the other end paused. "Mrs. Grassleby, I can arrange for a technician to come to your residence. Would this afternoon be convenient?"

Mutters had wandered back into the kitchen, foam clinging to either side of his mouth. The shoe had not been a substantial enough diversion.

"Impossible," Sunny said. She loved that crazy dog. "We have soccer and gymnastics and then a T-ball game. Is tomorrow morning possible? It has to be after ten, though, because of swim practice." She reached into the freezer for a treat. "Good boy," she said as Mutters sat up to beg for the snack.

"Ma'am?"

"What? No, not you." Mutters chomped the frozen kibble at her feet.

"Yes, ma'am. We can send someone late morning. But I must warn you that it's possible we'll quite likely want to take the Jaguar in for evaluation. Will you need a temporary replacement?"

"No," Sunny said. "We still have the Benz."

"Very good."

"Well, thanks for calling." Sunny picked up the stereo remote and clicked. "We'll see you tomorrow." She disconnected the phone and reached into the kitchen sink for a sponge.

15

Chesa Areglo read spy novels in her free time. The stack of DVDs next to the flat screen in her room showed a similar preference. Her parents, especially her mother, had tried to interest her in Jane Austen when she was a girl, or that tedious series about a red-haired school teacher in Canada. They wanted her to be a refined young lady.

Instead, when Chesa's class had a period in the school library, she went straight for the shelf holding Alistair MacLean and Agatha Christie. She dove into their stories, as well as others by John Gardner and Robert Ludlum. As much as she wanted to like le Carré, though, she found his books impenetrable. She would read on the bus, before piano lessons, and while doing chores, snatching a book off piles she kept around the house. When Chesa wasn't reading, she would imagine herself woven into the plots of the books she inhaled.

That's what got her thinking about her mother's mysterious sister.

Chesa's aunt Dulcinea owned a flat in Manila but was rarely at home and, despite her claims to be close with her sister, Dulcinea's visits were infrequent and unpredictable. When Chesa asked her aunt about her job, Dulcinea shifted the discussion to another topic; when her aunt spoke of travels, she gave few specifics. The clues definitely pointed in this direction, which made Chesa giddy. Her aunt—a spy!

Really? Impossible. And yet, perhaps. Chesa, being a practical girl, needed proof. But how? she wondered. I cannot ask my mother, because if my aunt were a spy, she would have a cover story and my mother would not know. Or, if she did, she would be sworn to secrecy and could not tell her own daughter for fear of reprisal. Chesa knew the ways of this world.

Nor can I ask my aunt. Either she would lie, and tell me that she travels because she is in international banking (a favored ruse), or she would fabricate some other clever story, used to put adversaries off the scent. She would not dare tell me the truth, if this is actually true (of course Chesa knew in her heart that it was), again for fear that others would find and torture me to divulge secrets.

Carrying this secret knowledge made Chesa miserable, so she tried to put it out of her mind. School dragged to a finish and after a languid summer, Chesa took a job in a grocery store, waiting for inspiration to strike. Her friends were applying or going to university, or emigrating to other countries in search of work or to try their luck with a different group of Filipinos. But the only ambitions Chesa had went unspoken, because she wanted to be a spy, like her aunt.

This was a hopeless desire. For all the books and movies she consumed, none offered specific guidance; the spies she encountered there were already well on their way by the time the stories began. Chesa's question—how does one get this sort of job?—was not answered in them. The phone book was equally useless: whom might one call? And the internet was so full of possibilities that she could not discern among the many sites which might truly offer her an open door.

Then, during one of her aunt's unannounced visits near the end of the year, the situation took a dramatic turn. Dulcinea had asked Chesa to go out with her for tea, and while the two of them were at a crowded café in town, Chesa's aunt asked about her niece's plans now that school had ended. Chesa had parroted what her friends were saying: university, to study for one's teaching credentials; Europe, to work in a hotel.

"What preparations have you made for this?" her aunt asked.

Chesa had hung her head then, for she had no details with which to respond.

Her aunt reached across the table to cup Chesa's chin in her hand. "Would you like to work for me?" she asked.

Was it possible? Chesa pinched herself. Was she about to be recruited?

Dulcinea poured more tea into her glass. "First, let me tell you what I do. But as I describe this work, I must ask that you keep what I say just between us. Can you do that, Chesa? Would you be good at keeping information to yourself?"

The girl nodded, very solemn. Her aunt studied her face. "I agree," she said. Then Dulcinea explained what she did, which confirmed Chesa's suspicions. Wonder of wonders, her aunt also thought Chesa might be of assistance. She could be a kind of spy intern, it seemed.

"You would need to learn some things, you understand," her aunt explained

Again, Chesa nodded. "I already know Morse code, and how to use invisible ink. Must I also study Russian?"

Dulcinea hid a smile behind her hand. "No, Chesa, I'm afraid most of these skills are no longer necessary. I have more mundane tasks in mind, like cleaning house."

Chesa had balked. Where was the adventure in dusting furniture or washing dishes? She could do that in her own home, as her mother often said. But eventually her aunt helped Chesa understand the importance of such work. Not long afterwards, the girl was a spy, just like her aunt.

Her first assignment was to work for the eccentric, possibly mad, Josephine Wainwright. Miss Wainwright lived in a lovely place, and Chesa was glad to be there, even if the reason for her job was actually different from the one she had explained to the woman when she interviewed for the position. Miss Wainwright had been looking for a maid, and Chesa, due to a web of connections spun by her aunt, had excellent references. But Chesa's placement was for the purpose of observation. She was to take no action, only to watch, and listen.

The girl had protested when her aunt described the parameters of this assignment, but Aunt Dulcinea was firm. "You must understand, Chesa," she had said, "that very little of being a spy is like what you see in your movies. There is not often much glamour. And so, my niece, if being a spy is what you crave, this is the kind of life you can expect: long hours of tedium punctuated by moments of sheer terror over a period of years where few will truly know what you have done. Do you still wish to proceed?" Chesa's aunt had posed that final question with a gentle smile.

"Will I need karate?" Chesa had asked, which elicited a brief chuckle from her aunt.

"I doubt it," she said. "Most of what we do is simply to blend into the scenery as we gather information. We rarely have fist fights or shoot-outs. Those are very good for books and the cinema, but most spies still go to the grocery store and visit the dentist."

Chesa was disappointed to hear this. "Then what is the appeal?" she had asked.

This too made her aunt's eyes merry. "To learn something few others know, to set right what has gone wrong, to thwart those bent on doing harm. I also like the travel," said her aunt. "People like us do tend to move around a lot, and we visit unusual places. We also have the most wonderful stories to tell, albeit with strategic modifications."

Dulcinea had turned serious then. "But now it is time for you to decide. If you want to go through with the assignment I have for you, fine; if not, that will be acceptable to me also, and we will never speak again of this matter."

Chesa had paused, weighing options. She could stay in Manila, and go to university, or keep working at the grocery store. Or, she could follow her aunt, and hope that her experience as a spy would take a more exciting turn. Perhaps along the way, she would find a need for karate, or a pistol. Anything would be better than the life she saw ahead of her in the place where she had been raised. Chesa longed for adventure, so she said yes.

"Very well," her aunt had answered. "You may tell your parents and your friends that I have secured a job for you in Europe that begins shortly, so you must say your farewells very soon." She pulled an envelope from her purse and gave it to Chesa. "In six weeks, you will fly to Lisbon where I will meet you," she said, "in Portugal."

Geography was her best subject in school. Of course Chesa knew where Lisbon was. "You will be working in the south of the country, and we will travel there by train." Then her aunt reached into her purse again. "This," she said, "is your new phone."

Another disappointment. The instrument was dull, scratched, and at least a year out of date. It also had a scuffed purple cover. "My phone is better than that," Chesa had complained. "I can take it."

"Your phone is not capable of doing what this can," Dulcinea had said. "This phone—she tapped the stressed plastic case—has a high resolution camera with night vision, state of the art encryption, GPS tracking, high-speed data transfer and a scanner. It can be detonated remotely as well."

This last remark had caught Chesa's attention.

"Not every part of the job is boring," her aunt had said, the corners of her mouth turning up slightly.

So after promising her parents she would be good, and telling her friends she would write once she had a new email account, Chesa flew to Portugal. She met her aunt and together they traveled to Faro, a town nestled in the southern corner of that new country.

Chesa moved into a strange woman's penthouse, squeezing into a small room of her own in a corner of the flat and spending her days polishing silver, shopping and walking Baskerville, the dog. Making sure plants that grew on the penthouse's terrace had ample water and enough shade or sun was also her responsibility. On occasion, Chesa would prepare meals as well, but often Miss Wainwright liked to amuse herself in the apartment's kitchen. Inevitably, after those episodes, Chesa would have a great deal more to clean.

When Chesa first came to the apartment, Miss Wainwright went out rarely. With the passing of time, the new girl proved herself reliable, and so the woman took to cafés and the theatre with greater frequency. She would always find the flat in perfect order upon her return, with Chesa in her room, watching the television or reading a book.

Miss Wainwright drew an invisible line between herself and the house help, and so she rarely spoke with Chesa at any length, but she seemed pleased that the girl was capable and careful. She even offered the young Filipina occasional instruction in the appreciation of life's finer things, such as she had throughout her flat, and especially in that one room with its magnificent view of the ocean. Unbeknownst to Miss Wainwright, Chesa kept detailed notes on the objects her employer pointed out, using the phone from Aunt Dulcinea to compile a photographic journal.

After some days had passed, it occurred to Chesa that Miss Wainwright seemed unconcerned about the threat of thieves and robbers, especially given all the expensive pieces in the apartment. "Aren't you worried that someone might break in or steal from you?" she had asked.

The older woman had not answered immediately, but instead invited the girl to stand outside with her on the balcony. "A person like me has a great many friends and acquaintances, Chesa, and not all of them are of the most reputable nature. I am completely confident that should any of my precious things go missing, I would be able to have one of these acquaintances locate my belongings and deal quite dispassionately with whomever had attempted to dislodge them." Miss Wainwright had looked directly at Chesa. "I would take any loss most personally, you understand." Then she turned her gaze toward Morocco. "Such a lovely view, don't you think? Especially from this height."

Chesa was remembering this conversation as she sent a text to her aunt a day after the summer solstice; she was trusting Dulcinea to keep her safe. But she also knew that she should be resourceful. I wanted to be a spy, Chesa reminded herself. I need to be clever and brave.

16

In the lift on the way to Wilma Ritter's apartment in center city Philadelphia, Max reviewed his plan. He needed to make sure Wilma was still willing to leave, and had not decided to dispatch Collingsworth and his assistant with something from her arsenal. It also fell to Max to convince Stephanie, the assistant manager in the Bell Tower's lobby, about a part she would play. He wasn't sure which of those two women was likely to give him more trouble.

Wilma was waiting in the hallway. "Ringo," she drawled, her deep voice scratched by seared vocal chords. The cigarette holder was clamped firmly between her teeth. "Come to see me off?"

Max grinned and held out a plastic sack. "For your journey," he said. "You like chocolate, I hope?"

"Long as it ain't got nuts," the old woman replied. "I'm not real wild about nougat, either."

"Then you're in luck. It's a pound of solids— dark, milk and white. This ought to last you at least until Cozumel." Max had persuaded Wilma to book a cruise that would take her around the Caribbean, into the Gulf of Mexico, through the Panama Canal, and north to San Francisco. She'd be gone three weeks at least, depending on how long she decided to visit with relatives on the left coast. Plenty of time for Max and his box canyon.

"So let me get this straight," Wilma said as she and Max settled into the living room chairs. "The fella you're wanting to catch needs a Babe Ruth card, and he knows I've got one."

Max nodded before taking a bite of the donut she'd offered him.

"And you want me to vamoose and lock the place up tight, so he can't steal it?"

"Exactly."

"Well then, how's your boy going to finish his business? And how do you plan to slap the cuffs on?"

Max brushed crumbs from his jeans on to the carpet. Wilma's snuffling Spaniel vacuumed them up noisily. "We're going to divert him from your place to another, where we can manage the situation better."

"But what about the card?" Wilma asked. Ash hung precipitously from the holder pinched between her thumb and forefinger.

"It happens that I've been able to put my hands on another," Max said.

Downstairs in the lobby, Wilma introduced him to the assistant manager, asking that Stephanie listen to what this fine young man had to say. Then Wilma left to take her dog for a stroll.

Stephanie ushered Max into the office just behind the reception desk and offered him a seat next to her desk. She stared at Max, her face impassive. Max surveyed the space, and the young woman's desk in particular. Photographs, a string of Mardi Gras beads hanging from a gooseneck lamp, speakers on either side of a computer monitor. Tidy stack of papers in one corner, a mug for pencils and pens. A pin-striped Yankees mug.

"Thanks for giving me some time to explain my situation, Stephanie," he began. "As a friend of Wilma's, I'm concerned about a possible problem with some of her, ah, belongings."

The woman across from him crossed her legs and smoothed her navy skirt. "Friend of Miss Ritter's? Until a week or so ago, I never saw you in the building."

"Yeah, well," Max smiled. "I'm sort of a new friend. Wilma is having some difficulties, and she's asked me to be of assistance."

"Difficulties?" Stephanie pressed.

"Security issues," Max said.

Stephanie bristled. "I'll have you know that the Bell's security systems are of the highest quality. Our residents have been completely satisfied. The building may be mature, but we have taken great care and spared no expense to make sure our residents will be both comfortable and safe." She huffed a little before settling back in her chair.

"I'm sure the Bell's security is first rate," Max said. "From talking with Wilma, I also know that she's delighted to be in this fine place. However, the situation she faces is somewhat, ah, sensitive." He steepled his fingers in front of his mouth and leaned forward. "That's why my firm sent me to provide her with an additional layer of protection."

Tapping a pen on her desk, Stephanie asked, "What firm exactly did you say you're with?"

"I didn't," Max said smoothly. "We're very discreet."

"I see." She scowled.

"But we are also very effective. I can assure you that if Miss Ritter is seeking our assistance, it does not indicate a negative assessment of the Bell so much as confidence in the reputation of our firm." Max was stretching the truth thin here, since he and Sty had been the ones to approach Wilma and not vice versa, but once they had made their case, she had seen their point. Thus, one could say that she had asked for, or at least agreed to, their help. In any event, Max's comments had the desired effect on Stephanie, whose shoulders dropped as she relaxed. Max steered back into calmer waters.

"We've devised a scenario that we are confident will eliminate the threat to Wilma's possessions. In the process, it will also remove from the Bell any further risk of this sort."

The assistant manager's lips thinned to a straight line; one eyebrow rose. "Is it really the case that Miss Ritter's goods are any more valuable than those of other residents?" she asked. "Or, to be more blunt, Mr. Starkey—which, by the way, is a completely ridiculous alias—is your firm's assistance truly necessary?"

Impressed by the woman's forthrightness, Max decided to take a chance. "What I'm about to tell you, Stephanie, is not common knowledge, although, to be perfectly honest (her eyebrow went up again), it's not an absolute secret, either." He looked out the office door then turned back and spoke in a quieter voice. "Wilma Ritter owns a Babe Ruth baseball card."

The assistant manager slowly sucked in air. "I already kno—" Blushing, she stopped abruptly. "One time, really fast, I—" She caught herself again. "I mean—"

"You've seen it, then?" Max asked.

She looked at the floor.

"Your secret's safe with me, Stephanie," Max said. "After all, something like that when you're a fan—"

"I have season tickets," she said, her voice nearly a whisper. Stephanie dropped the pen into her Yankees mug. "I take the train up every chance I get. I grew up in Queens and—"

In his seat, Max leaned toward her, fascinated by the confession a simple reference to baseball could evoke. She put a hand to her cheek, brushing a small scar there. "Anyway, when one of the cleaning women told me that she saw that card in Miss Ritter's hallway, I had to—"

Max stood and walked around to the back of his chair, placing it between himself and Stephanie. "Did you ever think to ask her for a look?"

Her cheeks colored. "She's a resident. I'm an employee."

"Wilma's a person," Max said. "A person who could use a few friends, I think. Besides, she an old crone, too, and she'd be proud to show off her stuff. Would you like for me to mention it to her?"

Stephanie's eyes connected with Max's. Light blue, he noticed. Rather large. "Could you?"

"I could, and I will. But it'll have to wait until August, I'm afraid, until after we've dealt with the matter at hand." He circled back to sit, then reached into his messenger bag for a large manila envelope. A single letter, a capital C, was scrawled on the front of the envelope.

"Now," he said. "Here's what I'd like you to do."

Trevor's cell phone rang. Before answering, he checked the caller's number on the postage stamp screen. Then he clicked the phone open and tapped a button to activate the speaker.

"Shropshire Magic Emporium, Billy speaking. May I be of assistance?"

"Is this the Magic Emporium?" a woman's voice at the other end sounded distant.

"Yes, ma'am," Trevor said. "Shropshire Magic Emporium. May I help you?"

"Well, yes, at least I hope so. You see, our daughter was to have a party next month, and we had arranged for all sorts of things. There was a pony, and a bounce castle, and wonderful food. And a magician. We were supposed to have a magician, that is. My husband wanted a clown, but I think clowns are too creepy, so I told him we should have a magician. He finally agreed, although he thinks we should have a clown for our son's party next spring. Maybe we will. But I still think they're creepy." She took a breath and Trevor interrupted.

"Madam, may we of the Shropshire Magic Emporium be of assistance?"

"What? Oh, I'm sorry. Yes, yes, of course. That's why I've called. You see, the magician we had booked has canceled. It seems he was in an automobile accident. Terrible, really. They said the car had been badly maintained and the brakes were absolutely shot. But who drives cars that aren't cared for these days? This man was no teenager; why didn't he know he should have his brakes checked? It's on the internet all the time." Another breath, but Trevor kept silent.

"Anyway, now we need a magician and none of my friends or neighbors knows anyone. A magician is not that easy to find these days, let me tell you. Especially when you live in the suburbs. We can't even find someone who can repair a slate roof, if you can imagine that."

"Madam." Trevor maintained perfect composure. "It so happens that we do have magicians associated with the Shropshire Magic Emporium and—"

"Well, of course," the woman interrupted. "That's why I'm calling. A day or two ago, I found a flyer from your company in our mailbox. Which is another thing that seems to be ready to fall down, by the way. It's made of limestone, so it's probably the acid rain. But anyway, I saw your brochure. I notice that you're advertising a special price, too."

"We are indeed, madam," said Trevor. "Our rates are most attractive and competitive, I might add."

"That's good," she said. "It's important to be thrifty. The last time we bought our car, the man said that if we would buy two at the same time, he'd give us a discount, so of course, my husband said yes, because we're mad about bargains. We have the brakes checked all the time, too."

"Most commendable," Trevor said. "Now, about the magician?"

"What? Oh, the magician, of course. Yes, well we need a magician for our party in August, so I'd like to book one."

Trevor waited for another barrage of loosely connected words, but it was not forthcoming. "Very well," he said. "May I say that our policy is to schedule our magicians for a preview with prospective customers. We find that it is helpful for a client to see what the program will be like in advance, so that there are no surprises."

"No surprises?" the woman said. "But don't magicians specialize in surprises?"

"Yes, of course," Trevor said smoothly. "What I mean to say is that this way, there will be no unpleasant surprises."

"I see," she said. "This preview, is there an extra charge for that?"

"No, not at all," said Trevor. "It's part of our package, the one you've seen in the advertisement that you received."

"Wonderful. Then what is my next step?"

"We would need to arrange a time for our magician to come to your house. You may have others in attendance if you like as well."

"Do you have any incentives if I book another date for one of my friends with your company?" she asked.

"As a matter of fact, we do," Trevor promised. "We offer an additional discount for every party you refer."

"Why, that's wonderful," the woman replied. "Now," Trevor heard pages flipping at the other end. "I'm looking at my agenda. Hmm, we'll be away in early July. We have the most marvelous cabin at the lake," she said. "We always go there over the fourth. My husband brings fireworks that he buys in Singapore or Bangladesh or someplace like that. He has to travel a lot because of coffee. He's a seller, not a grower, you understand. Well, I guess he has ideas about flavors, too. We go to the lake and set off fireworks and grill steaks and lay in the sun. He plays poker there with some friends every year, which I think is boring. It's wonderful. The cabin, I mean. So relaxing. The stress here sometimes is more than I like to think about. My husband says it makes me scattered a little, but I'm not sure. We don't get back until the eighth. Is there a good day after that?"

Trevor consulted an imaginary schedule book. "I have the eleventh open," he said.

She was humming.

"Would the eleventh be satisfactory?" Trevor repeated.

"What? Oh, no, the eleventh is no good. We have to be away that day and the day before. My husband has a convention in Houston. A coffee convention, can you believe it? In Houston, in July? That's nuts. But it's his business that pays the bills, so we go, go, go. Does July thirteen work? You're not superstitious, are you?"

Trevor's even demeanor was starting to show cracks. This call should have been straightforward.

"No," he said, through slightly clenched teeth. "Yes, July thirteen would be fine. I'll send you the appropriate paperwork for, shall we say, about 10:30 in the morning?"

"Yes, 10:30 would be super. Can you fax the information? We love technology here. You can use this number, our phone is so smart. Will your magician need lunch, or does he like coffee? I hope so, because everyone around here drinks coffee. All the time, it seems. Anyway, thanks, I'll see you then. Buh-bye."

Trevor cut the connection then turned to Mr. Cumin. The older man's eyes were tightly closed as he muttered, "Thank the gods that this is a burglary and not a kidnapping."

17

With the eleventh of July less than seventy-two hours away, Sty Bedford settled in to worry. He brought a cot to his third floor hotel office, hung a 'Do Not Disturb' sign on the knob and pulled a stack of old magazines from the cupboard. The mini-fridge was stocked with pot pies and beer.

He and Max had reviewed scenarios and contingencies by phone. "We need to get eyes on this guy, to make sure it's Collingsworth we're dealing with," Sty had said. "Foxe told me Phine has a stable of talent she draws from. It still could be someone else."

Max was less worried. "We know Collingsworth is in the States, because he messed up de Groot, right? We know Foxe has been passing information to Collingsworth about these jobs, too." Before Max could cover the receiver, he sneezed. "By the way, I wanted to ask you about that, since Foxe is also talking to us. Are you sure we can trust him?"

"Playing both sides is what makes him a good snitch," Sty said. "But on account of past events and developments, he also tends to tilt in my favor. So I'm OK with moving ahead with what we get from him."

Max sneezed again.

"You sick?" Sty asked.

"Allergies," Max said. "Roma just got a puppy. She brought it over last night and the thing left most of its hair in my place. Between that and Wilma's dog, I can't hardly breathe." He sniffed loudly. "OK, we'll go with that, then. But in order for us to confirm, we'll have to be where Collingsworth is heading before he arrives."

"Exactly," his uncle said. "That's why I want you over at Grassleby's place."

"Yeah, but if I'm there—"

"I'll plug someone else in at the other house."

"Anyone I know?" Max asked.

"Nope."

Part of Sty wanted to be back east, hovering over the field op. The other part, the more sane part, knew Max could handle this.

His sane part was crazy.

Josephine being in the picture meant that Sty could take nothing for granted. Sure, she was a continent away, but he did not doubt that she could pull strings even from a great distance. It wasn't like she could make his life miserable in just one way, either. There was Dulcinea's niece, parked in Phine's house, no less. And the daughter of his friend, en route at this point. The potential for collateral damage always put him on edge.

Sty shook off the pre-game jitters. The pieces were in place, the clock was running. Time to stay sharp.

By mid-afternoon on the tenth, Max was strolling along the sidewalk near the Bell, checking for suspicious activity from behind mirrored shades. He wanted to make sure Collingsworth and his partner were not lurking in some dark alley or windowless van. Once certain the area was clear, he pushed through the Bell's revolving door. Stephanie was behind the reception desk, talking on the phone. When she saw Max enter, she turned her back and spoke in a whisper.

Max approached the counter and heard her say, "Yes, I'll see you later this evening. Good-bye, Edward." Then she turned toward Max, her expression professional. She acknowledged him with a curt nod, handed him the key for the lift, then busied herself with a bouquet of flowers on the far corner of the reception desk.

Waiting briefly for some other sign, Max realized none was forthcoming. I am losing my grip, he thought on the way to the elevator.

Wilma was waiting in the foyer of her apartment, standing next to a matching pair of suitcases. The Spaniel lay before her, mournful. She held the dog's leash.

"You don't mind my beast in your car?" she asked Max.

He shook his head, trying to stifle a sneeze. "I've got a kennel in the back I'm sure Dominic will enjoy," Max said, surveying the apartment. "My sister loves dogs, so Dom will be well cared for."

Max checked Wilma's luggage: a full-sized bag and a smaller one of the same material. "Kinda light for three weeks, don't you think?"

The woman lit another cigarette, inhaled, held the smoke, then blew a pair of perfect rings. "I plan to shop on the boat. Do you know how long it's been since I bought new clothes?"

"No idea," Max said, grabbing the pair of suitcases. "Ready?"

She punched a code into the security console on the foyer's wall. A trio of green lights turned red. Waving Max into the hallway, Wilma pulled the apartment door closed behind her and locked the deadbolt. "Armed and dangerous," she said.

"Wait a minute. Are you packing?" Max asked.

The woman's laugh ended with a raspy cough. "I meant the apartment, Ringo, though now that you mention it—"

Max popped the suitcase's handle and set out for the elevator. "Too late," he said. "Time to go."

Behind him, Wilma said, "What about skeet shooting on the boat?"

Instead of exiting from the lobby, Max led Wilma to a rear entrance.

"I didn't know this was here," she said as Max held a door at the end of a corridor that led to the rear entrance. "How did you find it?"

"One of the doormen," Max said.

She nudged the Spaniel through the opening. "You're sure we have to be sneaking around?" she asked.

"For now, it's best," Max said. "The fewer who know about your departure, the better."

He helped the woman down a half flight of stairs, then settled her and her dog in the van he had borrowed from Roma. As they slid out of the alley on to the main road, Max realized he would breathe easier, figuratively speaking, once he had the woman at the airport.

He glanced over his shoulder at Dominic, comatose in the wire mesh crate. "You alive, boy?"

A brief whimper was the creature's only response.

Max spoke to the rearview. "You'll be fine."

"You talking to the dog, or yourself?" Wilma asked.

The next morning, a clear sky allowed the sun's full strength to beat down. Another July scorcher. Cumin picked his way across paving stones interspersed with moss, aggravated by the heat. Behind him, the rolling lawn was littered with people in khaki shirts and green trousers riding mowers or raking grass clippings. Each wore a black cap. Are these caps mandatory in America? Cumin wondered. He saw them everywhere.

Cumin rang the doorbell, surveying the house while he waited. Tall windows punctuated three stories of brick and stone; four chimneys shot through the roof. Multiple garage doors at the far end of the house, another set on the face of a detached structure that opened on to the circular drive where a gleaming black Jaguar was parked, in front of a van from the English Motors Group. Another van, emblazoned with the out-sized logo of a cable company, was parked closer to the main house. A pair of flagpoles stood in a circle of manicured grass and shrubs bounded by the driveway; other workers there were busily snipping and shaping. Ludicrous excess, Cumin thought. Typically American. He pressed the bell again.

Footfalls along tile flooring announced someone coming; then the door opened with an annoyingly loud, "How ya doin'?"

The loud, brash voice grated. The explosion of color on the man's tie offended. And his hair: did no one in these colonies possess a comb? Perhaps that was why so many wore caps. Cumin drew upon dwindling reserves to keep a civil tongue.

"Mr. Grassleby?"

"That's me," the man said, looking over the thief's head into the driveway. "You the guys from EMG? Listen, I gotta be in DC for lunch. Will this take long?"

"No sir, not at all. We've brought your vehicle."

"Great. Come on in. You know, I hate Jaguars. The wife, she loves anything British. Give me German any day. You find anything serious with that heap?"

"Not really. From time to time, the electronics of the XJ8 send a warning regarding needed adjustments. It's actually quite an advanced system."

"Yeah, maybe. But my ride, it hasn't seen the inside of a shop since I owned it."

"Indeed."

The two men stood in the foyer. Behind a door at the end of the hall, a frenzied dog barked. Grassleby twisted his head and yelled down the corridor, "Sunny, can you shut that thing up?" He turned back to the other man. "Sorry, where were we?"

Cumin consulted a work order he held. "I'll need to check your registration and sales documents. Then, if you'd be so good as to sign this, Mr. Grassleby?"

"Yeah, OK. That stuff's back in my study. As for this," the man grabbed Cumin's clipboard. "Have to read the fine print. Devil's in the details, right?" His abrupt laugh grated. "C'mon back."

The two walked down a short hall and into a paneled room where shelves were stacked with books and various objects on display.

"Mementos from your travels?" Cumin asked.

The man was searching through piles on his desk, distracted. "Investments, or stuff my wife wants. Business, too. Gifts from people expressing their thanks." He winked. "Sometimes in ways that don't always fit a tax form, if you know what I mean."

Cumin, facing away from the man, scowled. No wonder the American political system was in such disarray. If lobbyists were required to make laws function properly, and if people like this were those lobbyists, then the country got what it deserved.

Behind him, the reprehensible man was muttering. "Where are my glasses? Can you believe a guy like me has to wear them? Usually I have contacts but I was up half the night with that infernal dog. No idea what it ate this time."

Cumin set his thermos on the large desk and walked around the room, admiring items on the shelves. "What's this?" he asked.

The man looked at what Cumin pointed out. "Page from an early Gutenberg Bible, like I read the Bible. But it's pretty valuable."

"And this?"

"Fancy fountain pen. Japanese, I think. All I know is it cost a bundle."

Inches away from Cumin's grasp sat a masterpiece, hand-crafted in the 1920s for the Dunhill-Namiki group. Its golden barrel and cap featured a pair of finely inscribed dragons, the Japanese symbol for power and good fortune. This pen had a nickname—the Giant—and had been fashioned by Shogo, an artisan of the highest order. Cumin knew its present value to be just over a quarter of a million dollars, this extraordinary pen nestled on an ebony display easel in the home of a buffoon.

"This is interesting." Cumin was pointing to a print that hung in a space framed by built-in shelves. The shelves guarded it from ambient light, and there was no additional artificial light aimed at the painting. Klimt, Cumin noted, which meant this place warranted another visit.

A sudden crash from the back of the house made Cumin start, but Grassleby ignored the noise. He stopped shuffling things on his desk and looked over at Cumin. "You're a curious fellow, aren't you? Art lover? Me, too. Look, let's get this thing signed so we're done, OK?"

"Certainly." Cumin came back to the desk and pointed at the signature line. "Sign here," he said. Then lifting a page, he pointed again. "Also here."

With a flourish, the man signed—using a Montblanc, Cumin noted. How conspicuous. Grassleby then gave the papers back to the Englishman, along with the car's title and sales receipt. "Keys?" he asked.

Cumin examined the paperwork then gave the other man a baleful glance. "Mr. Grassleby, the English Motors Group policy is that customers confirm their automobiles are in acceptable condition before we release them. Would you mind coming outside to examine it for yourself? We want to be absolutely certain that you are satisfied."

The executive ran fingers through his rumpled hair and grumbled. "Look, the clock is ticking and time is money."

"I assure you, sir, this will take only a moment."

The other man sighed deeply. "Fine."

Cumin retraced his steps through the hall, followed by the other man. Outside, a driver sat in the EMG van, reading a paper.

"My colleague," Cumin explained with a dismissive wave. They approached the Jaguar and Cumin opened the driver's door. "Here we are. Do inspect the cabin that all is well, won't you?"

Grassleby slid into the seat while Cumin held the door open.

"Oh dear," the Englishman said. "I've left my tea thermos in your house. Do you mind if I retrieve it? I'll just be a moment." Cumin beckoned to his assistant. "Trevor, do attend Mr. Grassleby." Cumin spun and walked briskly toward the house. Trevor left his van to take up a position next to the Jag.

"Mr. Grassleby, a good day to you, sir. Would you be so good as to start the vehicle? We want you to be completely pleased." Trevor carefully closed the driver's door, and stepped toward the car, a human mountain that both kept the driver in his vehicle and blocked any view of the house.

Grassleby cranked the key, but the Jaguar only sputtered.

Trevor flashed a sheepish smile. "Most irregular. Do wait a moment, sir, and then please try again."

This time, the car started instantly. Grassleby revved the motor then let it settle into a quiet purr.

"Will you want a test drive before we leave?" Trevor asked.

"No thanks, no time," the man said from inside the car. "I'm sure everything is fine. If not, you boys can just come back, right?" He reached for the door handle. "Do you mind?"

Trevor paused a beat before backing away. "Pardon me, sir."

Grassleby climbed out of the car as Cumin reappeared from the house. He walked down the drive, waving a thermos. "Is all well, Mr. Grassleby?"

"Yep. You guys want anything else from me?"

Cumin looked at Trevor and then at the Jaguar's owner. That tie was particularly unsettling. "I don't believe so, sir." He tapped the thermos with his clipboard. "We have everything we need." With a slight bow, Cumin said, "It's been a pleasure, sir. And we at English Motors Group trust your driving experience continues to be a splendid one. Please do not hesitate to contact us should any further issues develop."

18

The man Cumin called Grassleby closed the door to the house and checked his watch. He slipped out of the dark suit jacket then unknotted the loud tie and draped it over the hanger now holding the coat. After extracting heavy gold cufflinks and removing his starched Oxford, he exchanged pressed wool pants for a pair of jeans, pulled a T-shirt over his head and grabbed a faded ball cap from the closet shelf.

Noise surged like lava down the hallway—a pack of feral dogs, ball bearings in a food processor, military invasion, and ZZ Top on stage all rolling together. When Max pushed through louvered doors into the kitchen, the cacophony engulfed him. The lone island of calm was a man seated at the table, silk tie loose at his neck, staring at a laptop. Around him, three young kids banged pots as an Irish setter, nipping at a moth, did laps around the room's perimeter. The woman holding a phone beamed.

"Those were them," Max said.

"What?" Sunny Grassleby tossed the phone into a basket of bananas. She pressed a remote's button and music from the ceiling speakers subsided.

The man at the table rose, went to a French door that opened to the patio and shooed dog and kids out-

side. Then he faced Max. They could have been brothers, even twins, especially after Max had lightened his
hair and glued on the ruddy goatee.

"What did you say?" the man asked.

"That was our guy," Max repeated.

"You sure?"

"Yep. The lawn people were legit, and so was the
woman from the cable company. She's still in the
basement, by the way. The plant rental crew first thing
this morning was fine, too. This last customer, though,
definitely our man."

"Any problems?"

"None," Max said.

"What about the pen?" the man asked.

"New one's a fake our guy switched out." Max
held a pen out for the other man to inspect. "This is a
Parker. Nice pen, but sure not a Giant. No worries,
though. We'll have the original back to you early next
week," Max promised.

"Take your time," the man said. "To tell the
truth, I'm not all that fond of it. Besides, I wouldn't
mind the insurance money." He laughed without
mirth. "Don't tell your boss I said that, OK?"

"Our secret," Max lied.

He let himself out on to the patio; his 280Z was
waiting in the detached garage. Max hung his suit
from a hook behind the driver's seat before jumping in.

Cumin's van was several miles ahead, but Max
had a heavy foot and the advantage of wide open
country road. He peeled off the fake beard and let it fly
out the window. Then he floored the Z and blew by
Cumin and Trevor. Watching the low slung sports car

pass, the former remarked about the deplorable driving habits of American young people.

Bedford did his best to look ahead several moves, but there were unavoidable gaps in the plans he and Max had made, holes impossible to fill ahead of time. For instance, they couldn't be sure of the order of Collingsworth's hits. Max and Sty had settled on a time period in which they were fairly confident he was likely to act, but his movement from place to place was less certain. So in the final days of June, they played out every permutation they could envision, and tried to plan accordingly.

After much wrangling, they agreed that Collingsworth would not attempt to grab three things in one day; there were simply too many variables that he could not foresee, from traffic to weather to lining up the supporting cast he needed. If anything was true of this guy—or of Josephine, Sty reckoned—it was that he left very little to chance. They also agreed that their thief would wait until the last possible moment, thereby reducing the risk of being noticed or caught.

"He got to be factoring in the significance of Pieter de Groot's lost briefcase, too," Sty reminded Max. "Collingsworth will figure that somebody else is in the picture."

"Which means—?" Max asked.

"It's likely to make him even more cautious." Sty climbed inside his adversary's head and beckoned Max to follow. "Remember: he already knows that in the past, Josephine has had irate owners after her. So if we're going to steer him, we have to be extra careful."

With the long holiday weekend, the Bell and both houses would be safe until after the seventh. Confident that Collingsworth wouldn't wait longer than necessary, Max and his uncle marked the eleventh and thirteenth as dates for his strikes. They'd scoured lists sent over by the Grasslebys and Lionels that showed scheduled visits from outsiders on those days. One in particular caught Sty's attention.

"A magician?" He'd called Marcia Lionel for details.

"For our party in August. He's giving us a preview, because I think clowns are creepy. Also, because our other magician had an accident. But it'll be after the coffee convention in Houston, so we'll be home."

Mrs. Lionel had more to say, but Sty tuned her out. He was scanning sheets from Phine's file. On a couple of other occasions, a magician had been among those in and out of targeted houses. Hadn't Collingsworth been a magician in the circus?

"We may have him," Bedford said to his nephew in a call at the end of July's first week. "Lionels are away on the eleventh, but on the thirteenth, they have a magician coming to the house."

"So how do we play this?" Max asked.

"Can you make our guy wait to hit Wilma's?"

Max thought for a moment. "Yeah, if she gets sick a couple days earlier. That would keep anyone from going upstairs."

By stopping in to see Stephanie before collecting Wilma for the airport, Max had been able to orchestrate the necessary change. In the assistant manager's cramped office, he had explained that Miss Ritter would be ill on the eleventh, so anyone asking for her then would need to return the next day. Stephanie had been reserved but willing, muttering about how elaborate all this was becoming, but Max did not relent.

He had driven Wilma to the airport, then seen her and Dominic safely to the security checkpoint. After that, he returned the van to Roma and collected his Z for the trip to Grasslebys. The point of going there, according to his uncle, was to make sure they were dealing with Collingsworth; up until now, they had only been speculating. Uncle Sty worried about tunnel vision, about only allowing one idea to dominate. But Max remained convinced that they were on the right track. He'd gone to Grasslebys to humor his uncle, but also to see how the Englishman would operate.

When Collingsworth showed up at the door the next morning, Max was elated. So far, their predictions had been accurate. But then as he watched the Brit work, Max felt a growing unease.

This guy had the confidence not to be splashy, and enough experience to see most anything others might throw his way. Hadn't he managed, on very short notice, to wrangle a van from the English Motors Group, an austere and well-run establishment? Hadn't he just walked into a house in broad daylight only to emerge with a pen worth a quarter of a million dollars, while in the process making the owner of that house glad for his visit?

Now as he barreled down the country road, Max was reviewing the past two hours. Don't underestimate this guy, he told himself. Between brute force, large cash, and sheer bravado, this crook gets the job done. After checking his rearview to make sure Collingsworth was out of sight, Max opened his phone and speed-dialed his uncle. Sty answered immediately.

"Kinda early," he said.

"Our guy got his worm," Max replied.

"You on your way home?"

"No. I thought I'd ride up to Wilma's, make some noise like there's still someone inside. She supposed to be sick, not dead, and there's no need to arouse suspicion too early."

"Good idea." The coffee maker behind Sty burbled as a fresh pot began to brew. "You'll call me if anything strange happens?"

"For sure," Max said. He closed the phone and pushed a cassette into the dash. Maybe after this job he could afford to update the car's ancient sound system.

Back in his Montana hotel, Sty tore the wrapper off store-bought Danish. Living in Europe ruins you for baked goods anywhere else, he thought. He sniffed the pastry, nibbled a corner, and tossed the remainder in the metal trash can.

Sty's knees popped when he stood; he needed a break and some fresh air. A quick walk around town would clear the cobwebs. He could stop in at Traders for a pecan roll, see if Audrey was working there this morning. The cell phone rang and vibrated on the desk. Max again? But it was an unlisted number, according to the caller ID.

"Hello?" Sty listened as a voice on the other end spoke quickly. "OK," he said when the caller had finished. "Got it. No, I don't think this will change a whole lot in the big picture, but we'll need to make a couple of adjustments. Shouldn't affect your travel."

The call ended and Sty snapped off his desk lamp. He really needed that walk now.

Fortified by a sweet roll the size of a volleyball and coffee better than he could hope to make with a garage sale machine, Sty dialed Max's cell phone. The first time he'd tried, while on the sidewalk between his office and this back corner table, he'd connected with Max's voicemail. The kid had still not returned his message.

Sty hit Max's voicemail a second time, amping up the urgency as he left another message. He scratched a layer of pecans off the roll and began dissecting the sweetened nuts with a knife and fork. A woman walked over with a pot of coffee.

"You want that topped off?" she asked. Sty eyed her ink—a full sleeve. The name tag pinned to her shirt collar said *Audrey*.

Sty pushed his mug toward her. "Thanks."

Audrey poured, then wiped a spill with a rag from her apron's pocket. She set a pitcher of cream next to the mug.

"You OK?" she asked. "You seem a little distracted."

Bedford blinked, turned from staring out the window, and refocused on the woman. "Sorta." He stirred cream into the dark brew with the wrong end of his fork. "Work stuff," he said, looking up at Audrey.

"Any way I can help?" she asked.

"Want to catch a movie later on?"

"That's going to fix your work problem?"

Sty shook his head. "No. But that'll pass the time until it's over."

19

More than an hour went by before Max called back. Sty was back upstairs at the Eureka, staring out the window at snowcaps, downing more coffee from a travel mug. He'd managed to connect with Foxe while waiting, but got scant information of use.

"What's up?" Max asked. "I forgot to switch the ringer back on after I left Grasslebys. Problems?"

Sty tore into Max. "You never drop out of contact during an op," he said, "unless there's a really good reason to go dark. Forgetting is not a good reason."

Max was silent. Good, Sty thought. He needs to feel this.

"Sorry," his nephew said, his voice flat. "Won't happen again."

Sty waited a moment before speaking. "Collingsworth hit the Lionels four days ago," he said, letting the force of his news sink in.

"Four days—on the seventh? That means—. Wait a minute. How do you know?"

"Last night, the person I sent over left a message for the family about arrangements on the thirteenth. Lionel didn't return the call until this morning. Turns out they'd had a fire at the house a few days earlier."

Max's heart skipped a beat. "On the seventh?"

"Yep. The Bach manuscript is gone, although there's a nice piece of parchment with *Claire de Lune* in its place."

"What?" Max asked. "How did he—?"

"Sounds like some neighbor called the Lionels at their lake place to say he'd seen strange people prowling around their house in the 'burbs on the seventh. At first Lionel figured their security outfit could handle it, but then he got to worrying about some of the things in the house that weren't exactly registered with his regular insurance company."

"Stuff you take care of?" Max asked.

"Us and some others," Sty said. "He's got an extensive collection. Picks a lot up from traveling in South America, I guess. So he beats it home where he finds fire trucks in the yard. The gazebo out back had burned to the ground."

"And the rest of the house?"

Max's uncle continued. "It's closed up tight. But a volunteer fire department is on the scene, and the guy in charge wants to look around inside, to make sure no sparks got on the roof or in some crack. Plus, there was a line from a propane tank next to the garage, for heating a Jacuzzi in the gazebo. They wanted to check an inside wall near that tank."

"The fire chief had an English accent, right?" Max guessed.

"No," Sty said. "He's a guy Lionel knows. But it was a slow night and a big fire, so he had a crew from all over. Lotta people with coats and hats standing around in the dark."

"He let them go inside?"

"Lionel checked the house first, then again after the crew finally left. Didn't see anything wrong, nothing out of place. So he called his broker about the fire to file a claim, locked the place down, and flipped on the security system. Then he drove back to the lake."

"So I'm guessing this guy's no musician, right?" Max said.

"Apparently he has no grasp of the difference between Bach and Debussy."

Max whistled into the phone. "Seems like we sort of miscalculated, boss."

"Yeah, but it's not a total loss. I'm guessing that bit with the magician on the thirteenth was to throw us off his trail, which means he intends to finish up today. He'll try to grab Wilma's card so he can blow town tonight."

"Can't we still put him off?" Max asked.

"Why bother? Let's close him down now, before he gets any more suspicious. You can handle that, right?"

Max would have to talk with the Bell staff before hustling back home. He'd also need some strategic delays to stay in front of Collingsworth.

"Yeah, but I'll need to jet," Max said.

He rode the elevator down and found Stephanie, to explain this newest change of plans. Wilma was away on vacation and not sick after all, in case people came asking about needing to get into her place.

"That envelope I gave you?" Max said to the assistant manager. "It'll be today, not the day after tomorrow, and most likely, pretty soon. And one more thing." He was glad that the Bell had internationally seasoned employees. "It's likely the person asking for Wilma will have a British accent."

Max started for the back entrance, then turned toward Stephanie. "You'll call me, right?"

She sighed. "About the envelope, yes. Right after it gets picked up."

Max tried to form a suitable reply, but she had retreated to her desk. Over, said a voice in his head. Never started, said another.

A silver minivan had its signal on for a turn into the alley that led to the Bell's delivery entrance. Max noticed it as he exited the parking garage half a block down from the apartment building. Two people in front, definitely not soccer moms. He made his own turn. Cutting it close, he thought.

Behind him, traffic cleared and the minivan turned left. Inside, Cumin stared down the long block. "Didn't a red sports car pass us earlier today, Trevor?"

The large man nodded. These American roads were full of sports cars. He wished his body were slightly smaller, so that he could fit the cabin of one more comfortably. A business associate had said that the BMW was rather larger, so perhaps he would investigate once he returned home after this job. His accounts would have grown considerably by then.

The alley they entered gave access to several buildings; a sign directed them to the Bell Tower's rear access. Trevor pulled the van into a parking space near the loading dock and cut the engine. Mr. Cumin was counting the bags arrayed on the middle seat once more, making sure that nothing had been misplaced since this morning.

The van's third seat was gone. Trevor had sold it to a junk yard a few days before, explaining that he preferred to haul items more than people, and that his garage was simply too full for something as bulky as a minivan seat. The man in the yard had given him thirty dollars, which pleased Trevor no end. Pin money for coffee and biscuits, he thought.

They'd needed space for the stove, a top of the line model, according to the young man who had sold it to them. Trevor had liked the stainless finish, but Mr. Cumin preferred black. They had paid cash at the cavernous store that sold lumber, floor tile and hanging lamps. Trevor had been fascinated by its size and scope. Mr. Cumin, predictably, had been disgusted.

Mr. Cumin had remembered to buy a dolly as well, which also was wedged into the back of the van. Now as he walked up stairs to the service entrance door, Trevor was glad for such sturdy equipment. Between that and the hydraulic lift by the loading dock, this would be frightfully easy.

Trevor pressed the bell push by the service door. A moment later, it was opened by a man in uniform. His name badge said *Dennis*.

"Hullo, Dennis," Trevor in his most cheerful voice. "Come with a delivery, we have." He motioned to the van.

"With that?" Dennis asked. "Looks like my wife's car."

"Busy day," Trevor said. "It's all we had available." Trevor knew that liars elaborate, adding unnecessary detail to make their story sound plausible. Vague came across as more honest.

Dennis nodded. "Whatever. You need any help?"

"None at all," Trevor replied, "So long as you're willing to pop this open." He motioned to the metal door above the loading dock. "We'll take it from there."

"Sure thing," Dennis said. "Hang on." The service door clanged shut and then the larger door began to creak. Dennis stood in the opening. "You want the hydraulic, right?"

"Yes, thanks."

While Dennis lowered the platform to street level, Trevor levered the range out of the van, strapped it to the dolly, and wheeled it over. Dennis thumbed the lift's button, raising Trevor and his crate.

"Lobby's through there," the doorman pointed. "You'll need to check with reception, though."

"Right," said Trevor. "Thanks."

Dennis faded into the semi-darkness of the service area while Trevor tilted the dolly and began to push. Mr. Cumin held the inside door and then led the way along a marbled hallway to the reception desk.

They had to wait behind a pair of spattered painters and a plumber. Finally, it was their turn to speak to the woman at the desk.

Cumin pulled a folded paper from his pocket. "Got us a fancy stove for some lady upstairs," he said, stretching his words into a lazy drawl. He read from a page he had produced himself using the computer and printer at an office store the day before. "Says here it's for a Miss Wilma Ritz."

"Wilma Ritter?" the young woman asked, trying to be helpful. The bronze plaque on the counter said she was the assistant manager.

Cumin squinted at the page.

"Dang," he said. "Right you are, little lady. Wil-ma Ritter."

"I see," said the assistant manager. "One moment please."

Cumin watched as she stepped over to her desk to consult a clipboard. His face hurt. A southern accent was facile to imitate, resembling the Cockney he'd worked so hard to overcome while at school, but it was painful to one's jaw.

Stephanie stood over her desk, mind churning. That puppy-eyed Starkey had said to give the envelope to a man asking for Miss Ritter, but he also said the man would have an English accent. Now here was someone who wanted to go upstairs to Miss Ritter's apartment, but he spoke with a distinctly Southern tang. She hesitated, unsure.

"I'm sorry, sir, but Miss Ritter has left on holiday. When residents are away, our policy is to deny entrance, except when there are specific instructions. Since there's nothing on our list, may I ask that you return in a week?"

With both hands on the polished counter, Cumin began to protest, but then realized he did not want a scene, particularly one that would be captured on camera. He would need a different way in. Catching his breath, Cumin turned away from the woman toward Trevor, whose hand was still on the dolly.

"C'mon Billy. Looks like somebody done screwed up. Agin. Less go get us a beer."

Cumin pushed off the counter toward his silent companion, who was jockeying the bulky crate for a return trip to the service area. Stephanie watched them turn the corner. A moment later, she had changed her mind. She snatched the manila envelope from her desk and scurried after the pair.

"Excuse me," she called down the hallway.

Cumin stopped and spun to face Stephanie as she walked up. "Yes, ma'am?"

"I just noticed my manager had left an envelope in case someone was asking for Miss Ritter today." She held the brown package out toward Cumin.

He reached for the envelope with a half smile. "Well, don't that beat all?" He tipped his hat toward Stephanie. "Thanks, little lady. Much obliged."

Without further conversation, the two men resumed their walk to the service area. Stephanie returned to her duties at the front desk, relieved to be finished with what she had promised.

The loading area was dark; the large metal door down and locked. Cumin used the illuminated emergency exit sign to find the smaller door that led to outside steps.

"What about the oven, Mr. Cumin?" Trevor asked as his employer sped down the steps.

"Leave it," Cumin said. "Something is wrong, and we must leave immediately."

Trevor asked no further questions, but pulled keys from his pocket. Cumin got in while Trevor started the engine. Next to him, the smaller man had torn open the envelope. He read the half sheet that it contained and then reached in for a second item. A photograph, Trevor saw, as the other man pulled it out.

Mr. Cumin looked through the windscreen at the Bell Tower's tightly closed service area.

"Someone has been here before us, Trevor."

"Then we've lost the card, have we?"

Mr. Cumin did not reply immediately, but read the half sheet once more, his eyes darting back and forth between it and the photograph in his hand. "Only temporarily, it seems."

"And now, Mr. Cumin?"

"Back to where we began, Trevor." He turned to his companion. "Get me out of this infernal city."

Sitting at his desk in the doormen's ward room, Dennis watched a monitor hooked to the outside camera. It filmed whoever came into the service area, and kept a video record of visitors. Dennis had seen the minivan pull into the space, and two guys get out: a thin, balding man and a linebacker, just like Starkey had described. Now he watched the pair drive away. Again, just as that young guy had predicted. Dennis pulled out his wallet, to count the crisp twenty dollar bills once more.

"Man," he said, "If I could make an extra hundred bucks every day, I'd be rich."

Dennis replaced his wallet and then opened the desk drawer, the big one. The cordless drill fit easily, along with other tools the doormen and security guards kept on hand for minor emergencies. His mind flitted to high school days, and one of his favorite pranks: the slow leak of a back tire. A smile flickered. And don't forget the spare.

20

Josephine had a headache. After a thorough battery of tests, the doctor said she was experiencing the effects of stress. Was there something out of the ordinary in her life causing undue anxiety?

Only my birthday party, Josephine wanted to say. When one waited seven years between celebrations, one developed certain expectations; one wanted to make an impression. Now, of course, all those were in a precarious state. Yes, the invitations had gone out and many had responded in the affirmative; she was pleased with the guest list. Yes, the party gifts were appearing, albeit slowly, for which she blamed that dolt Collingsworth. Hadn't remembered the American holiday? Needed more time to procure what he'd been sent to retrieve? She would fire him after this. He was not to be trusted for any future celebration.

Thankfully, she had finally found a dress that would not embarrass her in public. This being her seventh party, she had needed raiment that both restrained and flaunted the appropriate regions. She also had planned the party to start at dusk, on account of its demure lighting.

Naturally, the weather was awful. Wasn't the BBC predicting a dust storm in northern Africa? Never mind that it would be over before her extravaganza. The damage this would do to her flowers. She would have to ensure that Chesa was unusually vigilant. The girl would sleep on the patio, to protect her blooms.

Not only was nature refusing to cooperate, but she had been forced to fire the caterer she had thought would provide service necessary at such a gathering. The friend of a friend had taken ill at a recent buffet prepared by this very purveyor; a problem with the prawns, by all accounts. As if having to deal with Collingsworth had not already taxed Josephine to the limit. She could brook no further incompetence.

Disaster was imminent. Of course Josephine was stressed.

"What is that confounded noise, Trevor?"

Cumin's voice was beginning to irritate Trevor. He would be glad for a holiday once this job had ended. That would also allow time to consider subsequent association with Mr. Cumin.

The older man, expecting an immediate answer, looked at his companion's taut face. Trevor had only shaved once this day, it seemed. The shadow on his cheeks and neck made him appear more menacing, and Cumin was glad the man worked for him and not for an adversary. He started to repeat the question when Trevor cut in.

"I should say it's a flat tire, Mr. Cumin."

"Can you repair it?" Cumin asked.

"We'll need to stop."

"Then by all means, do so."

Trevor scowled. The traffic on this road was thickening. If they did not hurry, they risked being engulfed by a sea of vehicles that would keep them from their destination for an indeterminate amount of time. But neither could he hope to continue much longer with an unusable tire. Trevor scanned the road ahead and checked his mirrors, then stammered across the rumble strip to a narrow shoulder. He set the hazard lights blinking.

"Do be quick," Cumin said.

Translating his frustration to a grip that would have strangled the steering wheel, Trevor nodded. Then he settled his hands in his lap and consciously relaxed each finger before opening the door.

The offending tire was in the rear. By the time Trevor pulled off the highway, it was badly damaged. He lifted the tailgate to release the spare fixed to the van's undercarriage. As he loosened a bolt, the extra tire, attached to a cable, lowered to the ground. Trevor pressed the spare with his palm: it was very soft. Hardly a point to putting the van up on a jack, as they had no replacement. Nothing for it then but to wait.

Trevor circled back to the passenger's side and tapped the window. It lowered slowly. "I'm sorry, Mr. Cumin, but the spare's bollixed. We'll just have to wait for assistance."

"Have you any idea—"

Flashing lights appeared behind them. Moments later, a uniformed man was walking to Cumin's open window.

"What seems to be the trouble here, gentlemen?"

Cumin kept his hands in view and his words civil.

"Good afternoon, officer. My friend and I have managed to get a flat tire, and he's just now discovered the spare is also unusable."

"Hold on there, buddy. I ain't no cop. Part of the road safety crew, I am." He pointed to the stitched logo on his shirt, below which was embroidered *Tim*. "Me an' Titus there, that is." Tim jerked a thumb back toward his pickup. A man in its cab waved. "Some good Samaritan phoned in a while back, said they saw a van like this with a flapping tire, so since I'm in the area, I get the call to find ya. Can't be having you jammin' up the Schuylkill Expressway this time of day, y'know." He pushed a hank of greasy gray hair behind an ear and grinned.

Roving car mechanics? It was the first impressive thing Cumin had seen in America. The notion dispelled his melancholy.

"I say, Tim. Do you suppose you and Titus there could help us?" Cumin said.

Looking at the shredded tire, Tim scratched his chin. "Lemme see what we got in the truck."

By this time, Titus was out of the pickup, setting up orange cones behind the van. Once he finished with that task, he took up a perch on the guard rail, indifferent to cars speeding by. Titus unzipped his jacket and pointed his face at the sun. Tim gave him a thumbs-up on his way back to the van.

"Bad news, guys. All's I got is a donut."

Trevor perked up with the mention of food. "Is it chocolate or filled?"

Tim gave him a quizzical look. "Huh? Donut's a spare tire, one of them small puppies. This one'll fit your vehicle there, but you're gonna have to go slow. Oh yeah, and it'll cost you eighty bucks." Tim wiped his mouth on the sleeve of his shirt. "That's a deposit. All you have to do is bring the donut—he looked sternly at Trevor, who was easily twice his size—back to a turnpike service station for a refund."

"Done," said Mr. Cumin. He pulled a calfskin wallet from the pocket of the blazer hanging inside the van and extracted cash for Tim. "Now if you'll be so good as to bring it over, my friend here will install the new tire. The donut, as you say."

Tim chuckled. "I forgot to tell ya. For eighty bucks, we throws in a change for free." He whistled for Titus who leapt up from the guard rail. The two of them met at the truck's bed and wrestled out a floor jack. Tim dragged it to the car while Titus walked behind, lugging the spare. They joked with each other and tried to enlist Trevor in their merriment, fumbling with the equipment all the while. Twenty minutes passed before the new tire was successfully mounted and the van lowered to the ground.

"A marvel," Trevor said, wiping his eyes as he climbed into the driver's seat. These two were better than Monty Python. "Thanks to you both."

Titus ambled back to collect the orange cones while Tim threw the ruined tire into the minivan. "You drive safe now," he said, closing the tailgate.

Cumin wasn't listening. As soon as Tim slammed the back door of their van, he and Trevor spurted into traffic. Cumin reached again for the envelope he'd received at the apartment building, to review its contents for the fifth time.

> *I have the card you have been seeking. For an opportunity to purchase it, be at 147 Washington Street in Glenford, PA tonight at 11 p.m.*

As proof, the extortionist had included a photograph. The same photograph as had been on the flash drive the Frenchman had sent as a copy after the disappointing start of this present adventure.

Cumin laid the note and the photo on his lap and stared out his window as they flew by squat industrial buildings bristling with antennas and houses that were clamped to hillsides. So there had been another after all, someone who knew enough to intercept his original courier. But one who was not swift enough to beat him to the Bach or the pen. Cumin took pleasure in knowing this, until a dreadful possibility occurred to him. He unbuckled his seat belt and leaned back to retrieve a bag from the middle seat.

The Bach manuscript was sealed in plastic. Cumin studied the parchment intently, but without proper chemicals and magnification, he could not be sure. The Namiki pen was a different matter. Cumin had previous experience with these objects; his own collection contained one of lesser value but similar quality and so he was familiar with the heft and design parameters. He pulled the pen from a velvet pouch and then drew out a jeweler's loupe from the case at his feet. Careful inspection convinced him it was a Giant. He would stake his reputation on that.

So just the card remained. If it hadn't been for Josephine's specific instructions, Cumin would have gladly surrendered this in exchange for being able to leave on time. The job in Zurich weighed on his mind and he was eager for a return to Europe and true civilization. But thoroughness was a hallmark, essential to his reputation. Further, he intended to deliver everything that the one who held his heart desired.

174

The card. Perhaps his opponent had only been able to find one of the items pictured in what the Dutch courier had brought. Or, perhaps he only needed one. Inept, or simply not greedy?

While Trevor weaved through heavy traffic with grim determination, Cumin willed himself to desist from speculation. He called the airline to change the time of their departures and then closed the phone. There would be answers soon enough.

Max knew shortcuts back to Glenford that gave him an hour's lead on Collingsworth. If Dennis had followed through, he'd get to add a second, at least. That gave Max breathing space, but less than he would have liked.

As he drove, Max imagined the thief's face. That note in the manila envelope had gone through several drafts, but Max was pleased with the final result. Dramatic, confrontational and borderline arrogant, it would, he knew, prove irresistible. Besides, the man had a deadline, and the will to produce. Collingsworth would come, along with his gorilla bodyguard, and Max would be ready.

21

Mike's Garage was occupied. The adolescents of Glenford had discovered it made a perfect place to escape parents and meet friends who wanted to hang out, drink beer, smoke cigars and tell lies. Someone had brought an old charcoal grill, so there was a fire of sticks and busted-up two by fours for roasting marshmallows. The garage was large enough for an assortment of bicycles and motorcycles; a clutch of extremely used cars was parked outside, along the alley.

It was still early, barely dark since the sun set late this time of summer. Inside Mike's there was a lull in the conversation. Teens looked at each other self-consciously. Even the fire had settled to embers. Then a motorcycle roared down the alley and coasted into the garage, adding more energy to the mix. These newcomers, who pulled bottles out of leather jackets, were magnets. High fives circulated.

They regrouped around the barbecue, poking the glowing coals with sticks, shuffling to avoid smoke. The volume of talk and laughter began to rise steadily; someone switched on a radio. One guy squirted lighter fluid on the grill. Girls clustered by the dump truck, talking in low whispers and glancing occasionally at the boys. The boys, over by the fire, tried not to be obvious about their interest in the girls.

"Davey," one guy muttered to the boy next to him. "What time is it?"

"Why, you got a date?"

The first kid took in the dump truck, then let his gaze fall to the girls standing there. He lingered a moment on Lizzie, that willowy girl who volunteered at the library. Then he snorted. "Like there's anybody in this town worth it. Nah, I told my mom I was going to Crenshaw's to study, and that I'd be home by eleven."

Davey studied his friend briefly then pulled a phone from his back pocket. "Lizzie?" he said.

The other boy snorted again.

"Relax, Romeo," said Davey. "It's like not even ten. You're fine."

Bottles clinked on the far side of the barbecue; someone turned up the radio. A few of the girls drifted away from the truck and began to dance. A few of the guys elbowed each other, daring each other. One walked over to join them, then another, and then a siren cut the country song in half.

Blue lights strobed into Mike's through grimy, broken windows. A hulking police cruiser screeched to a stop on one side of the huge open door, shining its high beams inside. The cruiser's spotlight caught two kids who had jumped on motorcycles. They looked into the light then kicked their bikes into life and spun across the broken concrete floor into the alley. The rest scattered like cockroaches, except for Davey, who stopped to pour a bucket of water on the grill.

The cruiser backed out, dropped into drive and hauled down the alley in pursuit. Bicycles spurted out behind the cruiser, heading away from it, but the motorcycles, tail lights covered with duct tape, stayed in front of it until they reached the main road. Then they shot off in different directions.

The cruiser gave chase for a few blocks and then extinguished its blue lights, muted the siren, and turned on to Market for a lazy lap of the block. It was enough just to scatter the roaches; no need to stomp on every one. Keeping his eyes on the road, Archibald Davis patted the seat beside him until he connected with the cardboard box. Pudgy fingers located the Boston cream inside. Coffee from the paper cup wedged into the holder between the seats was still warm.

Back at Mike's, a lone figure shuffled into the now vacant garage. The long coat must have been sweltering on this July night, but its wearer seemed indifferent to discomfort. Of far greater importance was the litter of half empty bottles to be collected. There were too many to carry.

A lamp hissing on the side of the building opposite Mike's illumined the straggly beard and hooded eyes of the vagrant who frequented this alley. He hesitated, reluctant to leave the treasure untended. Then the man jumped like he'd been stung and loped into the alley. Moments later, he emerged from behind a dumpster with a battered grocery cart that he forced back into the garage. Bottles filled the cart, and then he stumbled on an abandoned cooler. That brought a squeal, followed by a hacking cough.

Nosing out of the garage cautiously, the cart's driver looked left, then right, and froze. That cop was turning back into the alley. The wizened man pushed hard, cursing the cart's broken wheel. Down past the dumpster another alley opened, too narrow for cars. He ducked into the shadows with his booty as the cruiser eased toward Mike's for another look, to make sure no more kids were hiding out there. That, and Archibald wanted some peace while he enjoyed the rest of what was in the box on the passenger seat.

Trevor and Mr. Cumin had watched this episode unfold with dismay. After their van's tire had been repaired, they had made slow progress until the interchange where several major roads converged. There, movement had stopped completely, and they had sat immobile for nearly an hour, trapped without hope of extrication.

Slowly the jam had thinned so that they could resume travel. They collected food at a turnpike stop— Trevor insisted that they needed their energy for what lay ahead—and arrived at Glenford well after eight, as the summer evening's long dusk was settling. Mr. Cumin had wanted to examine the rendezvous while it was still light, but as they turned into the alley, they heard a commotion. More cars were parked along the rough pavement than had previously been the case, too. Trevor had backed the van out and found parking at the curb across from the alley. They would investigate on foot.

When it became obvious the garage was occupied, they retreated to the van to wait. Their position afforded a partial view of the narrow lane.

"Once again, we find ourselves slightly behind," Mr. Cumin had observed.

"They shan't stay long, Mr. Cumin," Trevor had said. "I'm certain that these young people will be returning home once it's dark."

Cumin looked at his companion, amazed at his lack of perception. "Do you really think—?" he began, before noticing Trevor's mischievous smile.

"If they don't depart soon, Mr. Cumin, we shall give them a nudge."

"Nothing violent, Trevor. They're children."

Trevor nodded. "Of course, Mr. Cumin."

At nine-thirty, after waiting nearly an hour, Cumin was exasperated. "Time, Trevor."

The large man beside him pulled out his cell phone and punched in numbers.

"Dispatch."

"Yeah, hello?" Trevor's voice was gruff, guttural. "Hey, I'm over on Market, near Washington. There's a bunch a kids at Mike's old place, making noise and partying. Can you send someone down?"

"One moment, sir. Your name please?" Myra the dispatcher could be a stickler for details.

"Never mind that. They been there more'n an hour. Terrible for the town. Send somebody over, will-ya?" Trevor snapped the phone closed. "That should get matters moving," he said to Mr. Cumin.

"Let's hope so, Trevor. Let's hope so."

The cruiser had arrived on the scene fifteen minutes later, with Archie licking powdered sugar off his fingers. He had been down at the Sunoco when Myra came through on the radio, but since the call wasn't serious, Archie had not rushed. He filled his tall cup with coffee first, stirred in three sugars and finished a comment to a couple of truckers about baseball and politics being the same thing. Then he ambled outside and squeezed behind the squad car's wheel. Earlier that evening, a grateful citizen had dropped off a box of donuts at the station for Archie and there were still a few left.

He got to Mike's halfway into a Boston cream. From what Myra had said, this was just a nuisance call, so he hit the lights and the siren to put the fear of God into these kids. They scattered while Archie took another bite. He pinched a piece of chocolate icing that had fallen on his knee and popped it into his mouth. Then he dropped the car into reverse, backed out, and gave chase, careful not to jostle his coffee.

Trevor and Mr. Cumin watched from the curb as the cruiser flushed motorcycles from the garage. They were about to leave their van when Mr. Cumin spotted the homeless man through his binoculars. He saw the tramp enter and reemerge, only to return with his shopping cart. Moments later, the police cruiser was back on Market, coming toward them slowly. It turned and crawled down the alley, which made the vagrant flee the garage with his treasure. Then the dark vehicle parked just outside Mike's.

"Does this town never rest?" Cumin said.

"What's he doing?" Trevor asked as Mr. Cumin peered through the binoculars.

"It appears he is eating," Cumin said. "A donut, I believe."

"What sort?" The stop for a sandwich had been hours ago and Trevor felt gnawing in his stomach.

Cumin lowered the binoculars. He aimed a morose stare at Trevor. "Round," he said.

"I don't suppose—" Trevor's wistful voice tapered off. His tray of scones was empty. Cumin said nothing, but silently raised the glasses to resume his vigil. The policeman seemed in little hurry to leave.

A quarter hour passed with excruciating slowness, twenty minutes. Eleven p.m. was rapidly drawing near. Cumin watched the officer consult his own watch and then raise the flap on the box now sitting atop the cruiser's hood. Empty. Smoothing what little hair he had, the policeman put his cap on. Then he brushed crumbs off his shirt, hitched his trousers and unclipped a flashlight from his belt to sweep the garage for stragglers. Satisfied, he climbed back into the dark automobile and started the engine. He pulled ahead slowly, out of the alley to the street beyond.

Cumin exhaled. The police cruiser's tail lights disappeared; Cumin counted forty then nudged Trevor who was dozing. "Come, Trevor. There's just time to get in position."

His subordinate woke instantly. An odd skill, Cumin noted, but an important one for this sort of work. The two men closed their doors quietly and crept down the alley to Mike's Garage. Trevor entered first and, with a final check of the alley, Cumin followed him inside.

Max's 280Z pulled into the alley scant minutes later and parked near a dumpster. He pulled the canvas messenger bag from the passenger seat and looped it over his shoulder. Mike's place was a few yards in front of him. Sputtering lights high on the sides of buildings that created this alley produced wavering shadows.

Max paused at the garage's open door. Not much visibility inside. "Here we go," he muttered. He stepped over the metal channel and cut around to the left, straight into Trevor's fist.

22

Trevor slapped Max into consciousness. Waking, Max found himself trussed to a chair in the middle of the garage. The dump truck was still there, as were the oil barrels. Same place as Pieter de Groot got roughed up, Max thought. Probably the same chair.

Cumin was examining Max's wallet with the aid of a small flashlight. The messenger bag, its sturdy canvas shredded, lay at his feet.

"Mr. MacAllister," he said, looking over the rims of half-glasses. "So good to have you join us this evening. Where is the baseball card?"

"Baseball card?"

Cumin nodded and Trevor's fist connected with Max's lower jaw. His head spun; he blacked out. A bucket of water revived him, soaking his shirt in the process.

"Thanks," Max croaked. His face, where he could feel it, stung. "Such a warm evening."

"Let me explain how this will work," Cumin said. Max heard a metallic snap, then saw a knife waving in front of his face. Without warning, the huge man holding it plunged the blade into Max's thigh. Before Max could react, he poured liquid from a can in his other hand over the wound. Lighter fluid.

Max howled until Trevor hit him again in the solar plexus, leaving him gasping for air. Cumin grabbed Max's hair and yanked his head back. Then he shone the flashlight in Max's left eye, holding it close enough that he could feel the bulb's heat.

"Mr. MacAllister, your note proposed the sale of this baseball card, a transaction laden, no doubt, with myriad details of your own devising. I don't intend to negotiate, but suggest instead that you hand it over immediately and then limp away with your life and a story." Cumin withdrew the light and Max blinked rapidly, trying to moisten his eye. Needles jabbed his thigh, thick, hard and fast.

"Before we conclude our business, however, I have a few additional questions, so do stay awake. First, I want to know who else we might be expecting this evening?"

Max spat on the dusty floor, clearing his mouth of blood. He tried to draw breath to speak. Every movement shot sparks into a different quadrant of his body.

"I work alone," Max said.

"Most certainly you do not. The information you have collected indicates a network of size."

Max shook his head. "Let's just say that I know people who know people.'

The slight Englishman circled behind Max's chair. "But this particular situation. Surely it is no co-incidence we are seeking the same item?"

"A guy in France set me up. Said he had a client who was looking for new talent. Wainwright, is it?" Lifting his head, Max tried to ignore the pounding in his skull. His inquisitor now stood in front of him, and Max wanted to make eye contact.

This time Cumin let fly with a stinging blow that rattled Max. Then the Brit shoved Max so that his chair fell to one side. Max tried to keep his head tucked to his chest as he fell, and took most of the impact on his right shoulder.

Collingsworth's ape picked the chair up with ease and righted Max before the older man who stood perfectly still. He had regained his composure and spoke with an even voice.

"I'm sure you are mistaken. The person you've mentioned has all the assistance she needs."

"Apparently not," Max said, bracing himself as he pushed Collingsworth further. He wanted the man's full attention riveted on him. But no hand came whistling his way, although Max could sense the gorilla's eagerness to take a shot. Cumin stood quietly, a hand cupping his chin.

"Perhaps it has come to this," he said, almost to himself. Then he addressed Max directly. "No matter. What is important now is that the card you have allows me to complete my task and return home."

"Really?" Max said.

"What puts you in a position to question what I can and cannot do?"

Max tried to smile, but his lips hurt too much. "Haven't you been wondering what else I know about those other items in the photographs?"

This clearly piqued Cumin's interest. He motioned for Trevor to stand next to Max. The knife grazed Max's ear.

"I will ask you only once for an answer," Cumin said, his voice reasonable, his face impassive.

Max blinked hard. His fear was not much of an act. "Well," he began. He drew the deepest breath he could manage and blurted, "There was that thing that time—"

"With that girl?" A new voice rang out, louder than Max's had been.

Cumin's face registered confusion. Both he and Trevor swiveled simultaneously toward the other speaker, but the room was dim. All they could make out was the dump truck. Then movement above it caught their attention. Three cylinders, arcing toward them.

For different reasons, both men understood what these cylinders implied, but each was momentarily mesmerized. Trevor was thinking back to the last time he'd had occasion to throw such canisters: East Germany, during a prison break, when his responsibility had been to make sure the guards would be unable to respond.

Cumin's recollection was different. As a magician, he practiced a variety of diversionary tactics so that his audience would regularly look the wrong way when he was near the climax of a trick. Light and sound both proved to be excellent for this. He regularly experimented with different combinations, although he did not as a rule use anything quite so large as what was flying through the air in his direction.

Fascination held them immovable for a fraction of a second too long, and while they stood rooted to the concrete, Max, glad to be seated behind these two, especially the large one, lowered his head and screwed his eyes shut. Because in the next instant, the room exploded.

23

Fire Davis leaned over the inert body of his friend. He knew Max was alive by the pulse in his neck; Fire was less sure about Max's ability to walk, see or think straight. There was ammonia in the compact medical kit he'd brought, so Fire broke the vial and waved it under Max's nose.

Max sputtered, coughed, held his stomach and then reached for his thigh. He looked up at his friend. "Everything hurts, Orange," he said, his voice hoarse.

"Can you stand?"

"I'd rather lie here and die," Max said.

"You're a baby."

"You weren't the one who got stabbed and beaten by a Clydesdale.

"You try lying still in the back of a dump truck for four and a half hours," Fire said. "See what that feels like." He reached down to grab Max under the arms and heaved. Max stood, wavered. Bending his knees, Max held his head in his hands.

"I think he broke my jaw."

"If your jaw was broken, you couldn't talk."

Max stared at Orange, hoping for sympathy.

"Of course, you not talking is about like being dead, I guess."

"Good point," said Max. He gingerly rubbed his chin then probed his teeth with a finger.

"All there?" Fire asked.

Max nodded. "Far as I can tell."

"How about the leg?"

Max noticed his jeans had been cut off above the knife wound. A white bandage wrapped his thigh. "Your work?" he asked his friend.

Fire nodded. "I had peroxide, so it's clean. The wrap is loose, and you should change the dressing in a couple hours."

Max put weight on his foot. He felt a pulse in the wound.

"Good idea. I'll take care of that as soon as—" His gaze fell to Collingsworth and his accomplice. Both lay a few feet away, face down, hands lashed behind their backs by plastic ties. Their feet were similarly bound together. "No trouble from this pair?"

Orange offered a half smile. "Not really."

By combining a flash of light with the loud bang of an explosive charge in close proximity, the sticks Orange had thrown rendered subjects senseless for several minutes. They shut down a person's sight and hearing; unconsciousness was also common. Three flash bangs in an enclosed space were overpowering. Not lethal, but certainly disruptive to one's nervous system. Had Max not been behind the two men, he too would still have been unresponsive.

"The bigger one was stirring a little by the time I jumped down from the truck," Fire said, "So I tazed him. The little guy, he's out cold."

"Two sticks might have been enough," Max said.

"I needed to be sure, since I wasn't getting a second chance. Besides, how long those things been lying around your place?"

Max tried to remember. He'd ordered the toys a couple years back for a New Year's Eve party; these were leftovers. Orange was right—one, or more, might have been a dud. His head still pounded.

"Did you find their van?"

Fire pulled a set of keys from his pocket. "Big guy had these, so once I got them cuffed, I went searching. Silver minivan, just down the block. I ran the plates; it was stolen late last month. But so many of these things get jacked, it's not easy to find a specific one. Especially that color.

"Inside are bags full of expensive stuff. Jewelry, a fountain pen, bottles of wine, some kind of really old money. Other things I can't identify, like this little green statue—"

"It's a jade sculpture, eighteenth century China. Worth about three hundred thou."

Fire whistled. "Larceny, grand theft—should be enough to put these guys away for a long time."

Max's head was clearing. "No, Orange. What's in that van comes from people who won't press charges."

His friend began to protest.

"Trust me on this, they won't say a word."

"So, we just turn them loose?" Fire asked.

"Not exactly. There's still the matter of one thing these guys pinched that is legit."

"What's that?"

"A baseball card," Max said. He turned before Fire could reply and limped outside. His Z sat where he'd left it. Max unlocked the hatch and lifted the spare. *Still a good place to hide stuff.* He reached in for a slim metal case, pulled it out and clicked the tiny latch. Inside lay the card, swathed in plastic.

Back inside, Max bent down and rolled Cumin over. He tucked the card into the inside pocket of the Englishman's jacket. Max brushed off his hands and stood upright.

"You let me take the card because you were looking for cash—something about buying a ring? I told you I'd heard of somebody who was interested; I even found a way to send him a note, with a picture, suggesting we meet in town and discuss the sale. But when I arrived, he forced me back here, off the street and out of sight, and threatened to take it from me. Thankfully, you were in the area, checking up after your partner had been by earlier to shoo away a gang of kids here." Max paused for a breath. His ribs still ached. "By the way, did Archie like the donuts? I figured a dozen would be enough to last forty minutes."

"He finished the box here in under twenty."

"Probably started early," Max said. "But don't interrupt. You were in the area, heard the scuffle. You broke in, subdued the perpetrators, and got me to safety. In the process, I was kinda banged up."

"You've been through worse," Fire said.

"Yeah, but then it was my fault. This time it was these guys." He poked Collingsworth with his shoe. "You sure he's not dead?"

Fire was working on the EMT certification; he knew how to detect a corpse. "Ye—" he began. Then he shook his head. "Wait a minute. Did you say I was selling the card to buy a ring?"

His friend ignored the question. "I'm going to need all those bags out of the van," Max said over his shoulder as he limped out the garage door for a second time. "You OK to tie things off here?"

There was no storage space left in the Z by the time Max finished transferring Collingsworth's treasures to his car. Max set each one carefully on the deck behind his seat, wishing the Z had more storage space. Then he pulled out of the alley back on to Market. Twenty minutes later, he was in his own place, where he laid each item on his desk for a picture. After encrypting the file, he sent it to his uncle. That done, he downed four aspirins with as many fingers of scotch and collapsed on his bed. He needed a few hours' shut eye before the plane left.

Stuyvesant Bedford could not sleep. After the movie, he'd dropped Audrey off and then drove deserted streets back to the hotel. With a nod to the night clerk, he took the back stairway two steps at a time, hitting carpet that was thin in the center of nearly every tread. He keyed the door to his office, stepped inside, and kept the lights off. The north-facing window was wide open. Sty stuck his face outside for air, checking that the fire escape was still latched.

The moon bounced off snow fields still on the peaks, making Sty think of Glacier Park on the other side of those mountains. Sunrift Gorge, Logan's Pass, and Hidden Lake all beckoned. It had been months since he'd hiked those trails; the new job was keeping him in an office or on a plane. Again.

Sty tugged at the wooden sash to close the window. His brain shifted, back to Josephine. Absently, he drew in the film of dust that coated the glass: a series of concentric rings, then straight lines to intersect the rings with cross-hairs. He leaned forward, his forehead touching the bull's-eye.

Behind him, the computer chimed, announcing Max's email. Sty wiped away the window scrawl then returned to the desk for an account of his nephew's evening. The file only contained pictures.

Pictures. Sty enlarged them one by one and printed each on a separate sheet. Then he began searching the files in his cabinet as well as the data base his firm kept on their server. Two pot pies later, Sty had matched several of the photos with corresponding images from his firm's clients. More than a few of these had not been reported as missing. Then Sty really dug in, sifting through back channels and trap doors. More hours passed.

A knock on the door woke him. Mountains blocked the sunrise, but light was beginning to filter through the room's streaked glass. He rubbed his eyes, winced; the knocking continued.

"Hang on," Bedford croaked. He put both palms on the desk and surveyed piles of paper. An empty foil pan sat partly hidden under one stack. During the long night, Sty had identified another batch of the stolen goods not insured by his firm, each of which came with a handsome reward for successful recovery. Sty would split that with his employer, as per a standing agreement, and split it again with Max. A nice bonus for this job.

Sty opened the office door to Audrey, who held two cups. Steam rose through the black plastic lids.

"Saw your light on," she said. "Thought I'd bring these over. One for now, one for later. Ain't as good after you nuke 'em, but better 'n the swill you make here."

Coffee from Traders, especially hand-delivered, would jump start this day. He needed that, because there was still the matter of Josephine's place, and clearing it out before she did.

Orange's bandaging had held the leg together well enough. Water from the shower made it sting; Max wrapped the puncture again as soon as the skin was dry. Deep, into muscle. No hope of a marathon this summer. Jeez, just using the Z's clutch on the way home had been a chore. He stepped carefully into a loose pair of cargo pants. Fresh shirt, loafers no socks, the bulky diver's watch, felt tip pen, small pad of paper. A final look around the room before pulling the door shut. Roma would check in.

Max slid into the Z's cracked leather, his backpack slouched in the passenger seat. He had slept past noon but felt exhausted. Coffee and a banana on the way to the airport would have to be enough.

Josephine's stress headaches had moderated slightly; she had the Frenchman to thank for that. Renard had again shown himself to be resourceful, for which Josephine was grateful. As a rule, she did not care for the French. They had too many unsavory habits, their language was ridiculous, their snobbery legendary, and they ate snails. Mushrooms Josephine could understand, in large measure because truffles, the exalted cousin of the mushroom, had lately become an obsession. But snails, no. They reminded her of the shabby house where she grew up, near the center of Birmingham. Smoke, grit, gloomy skies, and damp walls all year. Walls where snails made trails.

Renard had found her a cook. Desperate, she had risked asking him, not sure that a man capable of unearthing information about valuable artifacts and handcraft would know anything about comestibles. But he was French, and the French had a reputation in the kitchen. She doubted this conventional wisdom, of course, although she also knew that French chefs occasionally killed themselves in a dispute over the ratings given to their restaurants. If a nation produced people with that level of passion, she reasoned, perhaps they could be trusted in this matter. But she still had reservations.

However, she also recalled that Renard had played a role in discovering Chesa, by passing along the number of someone who knew the girl was available and competent. Chesa had done very well indeed, so when her Frenchman—for she thought of Renard as more of a possession than as a person—had located a caterer with impeccable references, Josephine was willing to suspend judgment. He promised to arrange a meeting, and Josephine asked that she bring samples of her work. But no prawns. And no snails, either.

24

Max tried to keep most of his weight on the good leg as he stood in the security line. When he reached the agent at the desk and handed over his boarding pass, the woman said, "Why are you in this line? Business Class is over there." She tilted her head, then scribbled on the paper and gave it back to Max, along with his driver's license.

On his way to the belt where he would deposit his backpack and shoes, another security person waved him over. His carelessness with the boarding pass earned him a pat down and a stern look. Once through the metal detector, his brain cleared. Business Class to Lisbon? Perfect.

A closer look showed that his ticket also gave access to the airline's lounge. Very perfect, Max thought. Why hadn't his uncle mentioned these perks? Probably he had, during their conversation late last night, after Max returned to his place and sent the photos to Montana. But Max hadn't paid close attention, what with all he had on his mind. Plus, getting stabbed. Max would cash a lot of checks on that experience.

The lounge offered quiet space removed from the constant thrum of activity in the rest of the concourse, a concierge who only needed to hear a passenger's name once, a counter of snacks, and half an acre of comfortable chairs. There were monitors with current flight information and a separate screen that listed departure times for guests in the lounge. Max left his backpack in the luggage area. Next to carafes of coffee, he found a plate for fruit, nuts, and an oatmeal cookie. China plate, warm cookie. Max filled a chilled glass with milk.

A young woman was watching him from a padded seat. When he returned her gaze, she resumed reading the magazine in her lap. A news journal, or literary, but definitely not fashion or Hollywood. Expensive cross-trainers, Max noticed, low socks and a tattoo on the inside of the right ankle. Something Celtic. Jeans lighter at the knees and frayed at the cuffs, tank top under a half-zipped fleece, thin wrists wrapped with colored bands and a chunky sports watch. Runner? No, a swimmer, judging from faint green streaks in the loose blond hair. Frequent immersion in chlorine did that. Triathlons, maybe? One more detail, as he walked by: a ring of twisted metal—third finger, left hand.

A seat at the counter near a window was open. Max set his plate and glass there, then pulled out the newspaper folded under his arm. Baseball season was in full swing, the stock market was languishing with the heat, fuel prices were expected to rise by Labor Day. How ordinary. Max checked the monitor. His flight would board shortly, but with a reserved seat in Business, there was no need to rush.

The girl with the magazine was leaving. Max watched her gather belongings from the table next to her chair and slide them into a single strap backpack.

She left without looking back at him. Max sighed. Folding the newspaper, he stood, then laid the paper on the counter under the empty plate. May as well go myself, he thought.

Business Class had its own line, no waiting. Max climbed to the plane's upper deck, feeling each step in his thigh. Seats ran in pairs down either side of this cabin, with the aisle side facing forward, the window aft. Max had an aisle seat. A steward appeared as he settled into it.

"May I take that for you, sir?" he asked, indicating Max's pack.

"Not quite yet," Max said.

"Very well. Would you care for a beverage?"

"Bloody Mary mix?"

"Right away."

Max pulled out a book, and his phone to check messages and try for a quick chat with his uncle. The steward returned with a glass. Max handed over the pack, took a slug of the spicy tomato juice and switched on the reading light.

He'd opened the phone when a rustling on the other side of the seat partition indicated that the window seat was being occupied. Max sneaked a quick glance around the screen: the young woman he'd seen in the lounge. She'd settled, and was staring at him. Widow's peak, no make-up, hazel eyes. Check that. One hazel eye, the other leaning more toward green. Get a grip, he told himself.

"Hello," she said. "You were in the lounge, right? I saw you there, limping if I'm not mistaken. Are you OK?"

"Uh, yeah," Max said. He rubbed his leg lightly. "An accident. Collided with a sharp object."

"Ow," she said, frowning.

"Nah, it'll be fine. But I probably won't do any marathons for a while."

"You a runner?" she asked.

Max nodded. "Try to. I usually do a 10K couple times a year. Was hoping maybe for a longer race late summer, early fall."

"Me, too," she said. "But I'm into triathlons. Swimming is my thing, but I like running, too."

"Really," Max said, suppressing a grin.

"I'm Galena," she said, reaching a hand around the partition. Another tattoo, at the base of her palm. Letters, or symbols, but nothing Max recognized.

"Max," he said.

The steward intervened just then, asking the girl about a drink. She ordered a decaf latte.

"They make those here?" Max asked.

"It's really just milky coffee," she said, her voice low. "But I don't mind. I'll find a real one tomorrow."

"In London?" Max asked, taking a chance.

She smiled. "I'm going on to Lisbon."

"Me, too," said Max. *Lisbon?*

"That's nice." Galena switched on her reading light and opened another magazine.

Chesa did not think of herself as a nervous person. Ordinarily, she was light-hearted and steady; her friends from school would have said she was both dependable and fun.

But the past two weeks in the penthouse had made Chesa jumpy. Miss Wainwright had grown more demanding in her expectations, and her instructions had become increasingly complicated and confusing. Chesa was to stay out of Miss Wainwright's special room; she was supposed to keep it spotless. She should walk the dog twice a day, but only at night. Chesa was to sleep on the patio so she could water the flowers there before dawn and then cover them with sheets so they would not get dusty. She was to cook for Miss Wainwright, with food specially ordered. But often the meal she had prepared went untouched as the woman would eat at her favorite café. Add to all that the yelling and the accusations, the constant complaints of headache—no wonder Chesa walked on eggshells, trying her best not to offend.

During their conversation in Lisbon, before Chesa had moved into the penthouse by the sea in Faro, Dulcinea had warned Chesa that it might come to this. "The criminal mind is inherently unstable," she had said. "Your books, and especially those movies, portray criminals as masterminds who have unusual capabilities, but more commonly these are people suffering from fundamental deficiencies."

Dulcinea had been eating salad at the outdoor café where she had taken her niece, Chesa remembered. "They can be charming, so be careful you are not beguiled," her aunt warned. "Keep firmly in mind that at bottom they are sharks who will not hesitate to destroy you." She had smiled then, and ordered dessert for the both of them.

In her tiny room on the Portuguese coast, Chesa hoped that Dulcinea had not forgotten her. It had been hours since their last communication; Chesa had found it nearly impossible to be patient. She debated texting now, but then a shriek from Miss Wainwright made her scurry down the long hall to the woman's special room. She slowed upon arrival and stood inside the doorway. Chesa willed her heart to calm, her mind to clear.

Miss Wainwright saw the girl enter before turning to a paper on her desk. Chesa waited, staring out the window into the dark night. Across that wide expanse of sea lay Africa. Africa, Chesa thought. Will Aunt Dulcinea have work for me there one day? Aunt Dulcinea, or her mysterious employer, who works in the United States. She could not dare hope that one day she might even visit that land.

The older woman continued to ignore Chesa. The girl stayed very still, allowing her eyes to roam the room. Was there anything she had not seen before? That pendant hanging from a tree branch screwed to the wall—a heavy gold chain with colored stones bigger than the marbles her brothers played with—that looked new. So did a plate on the bookshelf, with funny marks and bubbly edges. Coins in a glass bowl nearby, also gold, misshapen and very thick—she had not noticed those before.

So yes, thought the observant girl, some new things in this room. Old things, too, such as Baskerville, dozing on his bed. Did that dog ever have a waking moment? Even when she took him outside, he walked as though he were asleep. What was the point of a pet if one could not play with it, or if the animal seemed completely indifferent to its surroundings? What made Miss Wainwright dote so on this beast who spent nearly every hour of every day curled up on this oversized, hideous jumble of lumpy cloth and wicker? Chesa had no idea.

"Yes?" Miss Wainwright spoke to the girl, but seemed surprised that she was there.

"You called me, Miss Wainwright?"

"I most certainly did not. But now that you're here, do fetch my headache powder from the bath. Then take Baskerville for his walk."

"Yes, ma'am." It was nearly midnight. Chesa waited for further directions, but as nothing more was said, she backed out of the room to find her employer's medicine and collect Baskerville's leash.

They had been in the air just over an hour and already Max was wishing the flight would last longer. A fruit plate, exotic cheeses, and Chardonnay had appeared shortly after takeoff; then the steward brought a steak, thick and bloody, accompanied by a memorable merlot and grilled asparagus with pine nuts. Salad followed. Max ate slowly, savoring each bite, willing the meal to last. He relished the pleasure of having someone else cook, and take care of the dishes.

When a dessert menu appeared, he studied it, wondering if he would be permitted several selections from the list. In the adjacent seat, the young woman's choice arrived in a fluted glass.

"How's that?" Max asked.

She pulled a spoon from her mouth slowly. "The mousse?" she said. "Passable. Especially given that it's airline food."

Picky, Max thought. This food is amazing.

"You seem to be enjoying the meal," she said.

"Yeah, I mostly do my own cooking at home. That usually means opening a can or deciding how long to nuke a plate."

The girl smiled.

"You cook?" he asked.

She nodded. "That's why I'm flying over."

"To work in a kitchen?" Max asked.

Galena nodded. "Sort of. A chef I admire from Paris is teaching a course. There's some chance of picking up a side job, too," she said with a slight smile before dipping her spoon into the mousse again.

25

After dinner, Max had reclined the seat and fallen asleep. A moment later, or so it seemed, the steward had wakened him and offered a warm towel, along with news that they would be landing shortly. Max brought the seat back upright and leaned across the partition. The girl there was reading.

"Did you sleep?"

Galena shook her head. "No need."

Max's connection to Lisbon required a layover of eight hours in London. He figured the same for her. "What will you do during the wait?" he asked as the runway lights came into view. Sunrise was lightening the sky.

"My plane takes off in ninety minutes," she said. "Barely enough time to make that once I clear customs. But you know how these things work."

International travel was new for Max. He had no idea how these things worked. He nodded. "Yeah." He stretched in his seat. "Me, I've got a few hours on the ground before Portugal," he said.

The woman beamed. "Where will you go?"

Max stalled. "Oh, I'm not sure yet."

"If it were me," she said, "I'd grab a bus to the British Museum. It could easily swallow a week, but even a few hours are worthwhile."

"Sounds good," Max said.

"If you do that," she continued, "Make sure to visit their antiquities collection, particularly what's come from Greece or the Middle East. Back in the day, the British liberated priceless treasure from their homelands—in the name of preserving human culture, you understand—and now they keep items that might otherwise be of national interest elsewhere."

Galena's hands were busy as she spoke. "Of course, they've returned a few things, but there's still a lot in England from other places. But then, that just makes it easy to see all at one time. Amazing, isn't it?" She looked directly at Max. "How one can rationalize nearly anything?"

Max realized he might not see this person again. "You know," he said, "Maybe we could get together in Lisbon for a drink or something. Or, since you know so much about food, you could help me find a good place to eat."

She laughed. "I won't be there very long, but maybe our paths will cross. Europe isn't that big."

The plane had taxied to the gate and stewards were moving through the cabin, assisting passengers preparing to depart.

"I hope your business goes well," she said, rising from her seat.

Max was less enthusiastic. "Yours, too."

By the time he had passed through customs, Max's eight hours had shrunk to less than six. Hardly worth finding a ride into the city. Max decided to camp in the Heathrow lounge instead, to catch up on email and grab a nap. Once there, time passed swiftly. Soon Max saw his name on the passengers' monitor, along with the gate for his flight to Lisbon. Later that evening, he tumbled into the Portela Airport, relieved to have the bulk of his travel behind him.

Outside the terminal, Max looked for signs that would direct him to the train station. "It's not far from the airport," his uncle had said. "Beautiful thing, near the coast. Go there, show them your ticket to Faro. Make sure you get a window seat."

Max finally saw a picture of a bus with an arrow toward a train. He slung the backpack in place and followed the pointer. A slender man wearing a beret bumped him as he walked along in a crowd toward the public transport.

"*Excusez-moi*," he said.

"No problem," Max replied.

"Ah, you are American," the man replied, his accent noticeable. "Here for ze beaches, *oui*?"

"Business," Max said, not wanting conversation.

"But you must try ze beaches. Especially in ze south. Zey are *formidable*."

"Thanks." Max tried to surge ahead without seeming obvious. He left the man behind as he made his way to a bus marked *Train* in both English and Portuguese, though he couldn't pronounce the latter. A short ride later, Max stood at the railway terminal, admiring the view.

Uncle Sty had taken care of that fare, too, and Max found his seat in a semi-private compartment. He did not have long to wait before, with a lurch, the train left the station. Max extended the footrest of his seat and turned to watch Portugal speed by.

The door to his compartment opened. A man entered, the same man who had spoken to him at the airport.

"Mr. MacAllister?" he said. This time, his voice had a British accent. "Your wallet." The man held out a leather billfold, then took the seat opposite Max. "Really, sir. When you travel abroad, you must be more careful with your personal belongings."

Max stuffed the wallet into a side pocket of the cargo pants without letting his surprise register. "You, sir, have the advantage."

"*Pardonnez-moi,*" he said, his voice French once more. "My name is Renard. But I am also known to some as Monsieur Foxe."

Chesa had spent the day polishing silver and dusting plants. She prepared a light supper for Miss Wainwright who threw most of the food away. After clearing the dishes, Chesa ate a meal of her own in front of the television in her room.

When her detective program was over, she returned to the kitchen, pulled Baskerville's leash from the hook there, and went to Miss Wainwright's special room. The woman motioned for her to enter. Chesa clipped the leash to the lethargic dog, a meaningless act as this beast would never run from her. A slow walk was all the animal could manage on a good day.

Back in the penthouse suite, Chesa watched Baskerville slouch toward the large, lumpy bed where he curled up and went promptly to sleep. The poor thing looked so uncomfortable that Chesa wanted to smooth the surfaces where he was resting. She walked over to the oversized bed and knelt, about to pat out the worst of the bumps when a shriek from behind made her freeze.

"Do not touch him!" It was Miss Wainwright, who had been invisible when Chesa returned to the apartment but had now materialized and was threatening her. "The hound does not require your attention."

Chesa backed away from the dog and his dreadful bed. Josephine glided forward, crouched, and ran her hands along the animal's grey coat. "Mine," she said. "All mine."

Miss Wainwright was having one of her spells, and so it was best to leave her at peace. "Will you require anything else, madam?" Chesa asked.

Josephine turned toward her with flashing eyes. "No, we're fine. You may go."

The girl backed out of the room completely and fled down the long corridor to her own, nearly colliding with the tall armoire that stood in the hallway. An ugly piece it was, and always in the way. She entered her room, closed the door and turned on the television as loud as she dared. She also sent her aunt a text message: *Are we there yet?* Chesa was not sure she wanted to be a spy much longer.

Thinking a cup of tea might calm her nerves, she ventured into the kitchen. Miss Wainwright was already there sitting on a stool, sipping from a china cup. She smiled as the girl entered the room of gleaming white tile and chrome appliances.

"Chesa, I'd like to apologize for my outburst earlier. My moods of late have been erratic I know, and I am sorry. Please believe me when I say I do not in any way hold you at fault. The party I am planning has simply taken control, and I am afraid it has made me behave badly.

"It appears, however, that preparations are nearing completion, and so in just a few days, we'll be able to celebrate in a grand fashion. I do hope you will enjoy yourself on that evening. To be sure, you will have a great deal of work, but nevertheless, I should think you would find it to your liking."

The young Pinay was not certain how to read her employer at this moment. Was her attitude sincere? Was this the calm before another storm? Chesa steered what she hoped was a middle way.

"Thank you, madam," she said, with a slight curtsy. "I am sure it will be a splendid evening and that all of your guests will be most appreciative."

At this, Josephine smiled. "Yes, I expect you are correct," she said. "It will be a most memorable event." She raised the tea cup.

"Madam?" Chesa wanted to tread gingerly now.

"Yes?"

"Before I went out with Baskerville, someone rang on the telephone. I tried to locate you, but did not hear you answer my call. It was the French man, saying that the caterer you requested would be available for a consultation." Chesa cringed as she finished, not sure whether Miss Wainwright would erupt again.

Instead the older woman laughed gently. "There, you see? All the pieces are fitting together perfectly." She tipped the pitcher, releasing a thin stream of milk into her cup. A single lump of sugar followed, along with another longer pour from the teapot.

"Did Monsieur Renard say at what time this person would be able to meet?"

"Yes, madam. Tomorrow, at three o'clock in the afternoon. He will bring her to La Sepia." La Sepia was one of Miss Wainwright's preferred cafés.

"Very good," the woman replied. "Though I think it passing strange for a caterer to meet at a restaurant. Did Renard also find this peculiar?"

"He said nothing of it to me," Chesa said.

"We shall have coffee and biscotti at La Sepia to discuss terms," Josephine declared. "Afterwards this person may take me to the shop where the food will be prepared."

"Yes, madam." Chesa was relieved to finish this exchange without an explosion. "Will there be anything else?"

"Please take Baskerville a drink." She stirred her cup. "You know how he adores champagne."

26

Sty had compiled a list of what his firm had lost over the past year. To this he added pictures and notes cajoled from acquaintances in the same line of work who were experiencing similar trauma. Not everything was Josephine's doing, of course, but Sty figured a sizeable portion of this batch had found its way into her hands. Phine would give some of that away to her party guests, but Sty reckoned that she'd also keep some for herself. Narcissists like Phine needed to be surrounded by evidence of their own brilliance.

Poring over data at his desk, Sty heard another possibility knocking at his brain. What if the party was more of a cover, an opportunity for that madwoman to gather high rollers, show off what she'd nicked, and advertise her wares?

By now, Josephine certainly had a back room full of treasure: would she slip away from the festivities with potential clients and offer to sell pieces from her stash, or take orders for other items? The more Sty mused on this, the more sense it made. Phine simply could not give everything away, or blow too much into the next century; she needed a revenue stream to support her lavish lifestyle, right? Bedford sat back in his desk chair and whistled. Maybe the old girl wasn't such a loon after all.

He paged through the thick file again, then encrypted the whole lot for an email to Max. If his suspicions were grounded, the flat in Faro would be loaded. And crazy or not, Josephine wasn't stupid. The woman would have a fair bit secreted away somewhere. But that was why he'd sent Max. The kid was good at finding things.

Sty added a few notes of explanation for some of the stranger objects, so that Max wouldn't overlook what might have seemed simply ugly. Then just before hitting SEND, Bedford paused. The catalog he was shipping to his nephew contained information that would be of great interest to others. Sty weighed the risks, then pressed the button. The kid was canny; he'd be careful.

"I have a message for you from Monsieur Bedford," Renard said.

Sitting in the railway car, Max kept his face blank. Renard, aka Foxe, was the guy his uncle relied on for information about Josephine's movements and acquisitions. He was also in regular communication with Collingsworth, although that, thanks to Orange, was about to be interrupted. Still, Renard had his own agenda, and would most likely look out only for himself. How far do you trust a person like that?

"What message?" Max asked.

"He wishes to convey that Madame Josephine will have a considerable collection of goods both on display and secreted away. I believe he is to send you some type of directory?" Renard's gaze flitted to the backpack on the shelf above Max, then smoothly returned for eye contact with the young man.

Max purposely ignored the other man's interest in his bag. "He wanted you to tell me something I already know?" Max fully expected that Josephine Wainwright would not make his job easy; he also found suspicions about the Frenchman mounting.

Renard smiled. "Very well. The message also is this. The colonel also has a strong suspicion that Josephine may be planning fireworks for her birthday."

"Fireworks?"

"A grand finale to her seventh seventh-year party. A very big boom." Renard spread his hands and made the sound of an explosion.

"In other words, part of this operation involves finding a bomb?"

The French Englishman nodded his head. "I should expect a rather large bomb. She may not use it, but one never knows. And lately, monsieur, I must say that madam Josephine has become more unstable."

"Noted," Max said. Ordinarily, explosives did not trouble him. So long as they were handled properly and treated with respect, there was little need for alarm. But such materials in the hands of unstable people—that created variables.

"Is there anything else?" Max asked.

"Just this. The colonel wanted me to see the pictures he sent you."

In the airline lounge at Heathrow, Max had downloaded a large file from his uncle. The laser printer in the lounge's business suite had produced a sheaf of documents that Max had studied before stuffing it between the shirts in his backpack. Now, sitting with Renard, Max had a sense for that document's value to one who was both a collector and a fence. He coughed, stalling for time to think.

"The colonel?" Max said. "That's the second time you've said that."

Renard turned to watch the scenery flying past. He spoke to the glass. "Before this man was your uncle, we served together. I owe him—" the man's voice tapered off into a silence Max did not break.

He wanted to trust this guy, but just in case, Max lied. "I still need to check my email. Figured I'd do that at the hotel. Can we meet tomorrow?"

The man across from him nodded. "*Certainement*. I know a place to meet for coffee."

"Fine," Max said. "Now, I have a question."

"Yes?" Renard crossed his legs and clasped both hands over one knee.

"What happens once I find the items? Am I supposed to take them back on the airplane as luggage?"

The Frenchman smiled. "Not at all. Surely you understand that there would be far more than one could place in a suitcase. Besides that, the items would undoubtedly raise many uncomfortable questions from customs officials. No, Monsieur Bedford has arranged for another person to handle the shipping. An expediter, you might say."

"A person you know?" Max asked Renard.

"One who will make contact with you."

They disembarked at the station in Faro. Max was dazzled by the surroundings. The few buses and trains he had used back home went in and out of urban centers, dingy places thronged by nervous travelers. He'd never seen stations so near the ocean, especially as the sun was setting. Beside him, Renard was speaking in a low murmur.

"Remember what I told you. Tomorrow afternoon at three, Josephine will be occupied. You will have less than two hours to locate and remove the goods."

Turning to ask about further contact with Renard, Max found that the man had dissolved into the crowd on the platform. In the gathering dusk, Max shrugged. He would find the hotel his uncle had reserved, check in, and then wander the town in search of a meal. Tomorrow he could stroll the beach, probably at sunrise, since jet lag would have kicked in by then. Then coffee with Renard, and over to Josephine's to grab the stuff there. After that, he'd join Renard again for the plane out of Faro back to London. Renard would stay in England, to resume his life as Mr. Foxe. Max would continue on home after a hop across the pond.

Max tried to pay attention as he strolled down the street. He wouldn't be here long; he wanted to absorb the local color. Perhaps one day, after this job was over, he could return.

Fire Davis still wasn't sure what had happened.

After Max roared off in his car, the earnest cop had waited until the crooks had regained consciousness. Then he bundled them into his cruiser, took them to the Glenford Police Department station, and ushered the men into a small holding cell. Fire decided to spend the night in the adjacent office and wait until morning before trying to sort things out. By then there would be a supervisor available who could advise him as to next steps for handling the pair of foreigners.

But shortly before dawn, three men had entered the station, to talk with Fire. The oldest one, with a full beard more salt than pepper, was clearly in charge. He flashed a badge and explained that the men Fire was detaining were big fish, wanted by agencies of somewhat more importance than the Glenford Police Department. This gentleman was neither condescending nor patronizing, but very firm, and persuasive. Fire had released the prisoners to his custody after signing official documents and being assured that they would be properly handled.

On the one hand, Fire had been looking forward to what would surely have been a career milestone. The capture of international criminals in this sleepy town had national media written all over it. On the other, he was fine letting others handle the paperwork. Besides, now that Max had planted that idea about a ring, Fire was finding himself more than a little distracted. He didn't need the added burden of celebrity.

So he watched the two Englishmen depart in the custody of the older man and the pair of officers who had come with him. They sped off in a black panel van, which meant Fire could lock up the station and go home for a few hours before his shift later that day.

As the van pulled away from the Glenford police station, Bedford Stuyvesant turned to face the men in the middle seat. The driver, who had remained with the van while the others went inside, paid attention to the road; two other men in the third row of seats paid attention to everything else. Cumin and Trevor, who occupied that middle row, wore manacles attached to a steel band around their waists. Ankle chains ran through steel loops bolted to the vehicle's floor.

"Let me tell you what is about to happen," Sty said in a level voice. "After a brief stop at the airport, you will be taken to Baltimore Harbor, where a cruise ship departs for England later today. You will be passengers, along with these three tour guides. They will make certain your voyage is without incident and that you arrive at your destination in good order.

"Upon disembarking, you will need new careers because your faces will be on watch lists for every law enforcement agency on both sides of the equator. In addition, I have notified a different network of professional acquaintances as to your activities and skills. They will also receive detailed descriptions and photographs. Your days as independent contractors in this particular line of work are over.

"Finally, should you wonder about the fate of your employer, she will be presented with similar options." Sty paused. "'Options' is perhaps too wide a word, but you take my meaning. Very shortly she too will be in the market for a new place to live and new ways to spend her time."

Mr. Cumin tried to maintain a stiff upper lip. He'd had a good run, but now the tent was being struck and it was time to move on. For him, finding other employment would be trivial; of that he was certain. Moreover, his accounts were so widely scattered that even these gentlemen would not have been able to locate all of them on short notice. All he needed was access to a computer terminal, which perhaps could be arranged on the boat.

Far more grievous was the news that Josephine had also been targeted. She would no doubt blame him, and rightly so. He had failed her, despite his best efforts, and his penalty would be unrequited love for the rest of his life. Darkness descended as Cumin sat awash in melancholy.

Trevor was more optimistic. He had been increasingly uneasy about the partnership with Mr. Cumin, and present circumstances simply confirmed the value of other outlets for his interests and abilities. There would be time to ponder his own options during the voyage, a trip about which he suddenly felt happy anticipation. As he understood it, cruise ships had buffet lines that never closed.

Ocean breezes wafted in through open patio doors that led on to a narrow balcony. Every room in this small Portuguese hotel facing the sea had such balconies, linked one to the other on each floor, where guests could enjoy morning croissants or an evening aperitif. Max had fallen into the comfortable bed after dinner to sleep soundly, but in the early morning hours, well before sunrise, he woke to what he thought was a woman's voice. It seemed she was shouting, from his balcony, something like 'Scott, are you OK? Scotty?'

He'd stirred, opened an eye. Was something moving near the chair where he'd set his backpack? Max rubbed his temples. His mind was fuzzy from the time change and too much sangria at supper. It was dark. Max felt for the papers tucked into his pillowcase, pulled the light coverlet up to his chin, and rolled over. He'd check more thoroughly in the morning.

27

Chesa was watching television when Miss Wainwright left to meet the caterer at La Sepia. The girl wanted to stay out of her employer's line of vision as much as possible, particularly on this day. She was afraid her face might betray a secret.

Aunt Dulcinea had sent her a text in Tagalog the previous evening: *Tomorrow is the first day of the rest of your life.* Chesa understood. She would be leaving the apartment today, and Faro, and probably Portugal, forever. Chesa was not sure if her aunt would place her as a spy for another assignment or if she would have to go back home to Manila. She would need work of some kind, as she did not yet have a Swiss bank account, something every member of the trade had access to in case of emergency. Perhaps one needed to be a spy for many years before one opened such an account. Chesa would probably never know.

When the bell at the apartment's door rang, she jumped. Then she turned off the television and stood, surveying her tiny room. Was there anything here she would miss? She scurried down the dim corridor, brushing against the annoying armoire. For all the space Miss Wainwright had in this penthouse, why could she not find another place for this piece of furniture? Perhaps it was too ugly to be in full view. It must have sentimental value, Chesa reasoned.

She opened the door to a young man in jeans and a yellow shirt with even brighter flowers. He wore an incandescent orange cap with mirrored sunglasses perched above the bill.

"Hi," he said. "I'm Richard Starkey. I called about a set of dishes you had for sale?"

He stood next to a wheeled cart stacked with cardboard boxes marked 'Fragile'.

"Yes, please come in." Chesa held the door wide. "It's right through here," she said. She led the young man to the back of the apartment, to Miss Wainwright's special room.

"As you can see," she said, "Everything you need is here."

Max scanned the space. "Know anything about packing?"

Chesa nodded, staring into his kind eyes. With nothing of her own except a few books, she wanted to ask where they were going, and whether this nice boy might be taking her with him, perhaps to Florida. She had seen pictures of Disney World on television and she hoped—.

But he walked past her, further into the room. Then he pulled a sheaf of paper from the satchel he carried.

"Good," he said over his shoulder. "Then bring that cart down here and you can start filling boxes."

While Chesa went back to the foyer to collect the cart, Max began comparing the pictures on his pages with what he saw on display in this room. Very quickly he matched more than a dozen objects, pulling them from walls and shelves.

Chesa had returned and Max waved at the table where he had assembled Josephine's ill-gotten gain. "There's packing paper in the boxes. Wrap this stuff as carefully as you can, but be quick."

The girl nodded, not speaking. Her hands flew, taking care with objects she had dusted on a daily basis. Some were so beautiful, others quite strange. It felt odd, to be removing each item from its particular place. But she did not ask questions.

Max swept the room again with his eyes. "Something's not right," he muttered.

"Excuse me?" Chesa ventured a brief remark. She did not wish to seem ignorant around one who was so clearly a professional spy.

He folded the papers and stuffed them into a back pocket. "Is there anywhere else Josephine would keep valuables?"

She bit her lower lip. "There are some paintings and little statues in other rooms."

"Then she's got a hiding place," Max muttered. He checked his watch: nearly twenty-five minutes had elapsed. He could not count on Josephine to linger over her afternoon coffee and conversation once business had been transacted.

"Any closets? Rooms she forbids you to enter?"

"Closets, yes, but for clothing, or cleaning supplies. I am in and out of them nearly every day. And no other rooms."

Max scanned the bookshelves in Josephine's *sanctum sanctorum*, then went to one large case and began pulling out volumes at random. He did this is several spots around the room. "No safe here," he said. "But she would need something bigger than a safe to keep all the rest of this stuff." Without another word, he darted out of Josephine's study.

Chesa found him in the kitchen, rummaging through cupboards.

"Only food and pots," she said.

Max looked at her from behind a pantry door. "Her bedroom?"

"This way," Chesa said, leading him to the far end of the apartment, a side she rarely visited.

Josephine's room was spartan: a large mattress suspended on an iron stand in the middle of the room, facing seaside windows; chiffarobe; a closet of dresses and many shoes; a bathroom en suite. But no secret compartments, no hidden panels.

Time was running.

"What's at the other end?" Max asked.

"A bedroom for guests, which is always empty, and my room."

"Show me."

The two of them sprinted down the hall. Max ducked into the guest room behind Chesa. This closet was also empty. Then he yanked off the bed's comforter. Using a knife clipped at his belt, Max slashed the mattress, confirming that it was stuffed only with foam. They scooted out of the doorway with the Filipina in front. She swerved to miss the armoire, but Max collided with a wooden corner.

Nothing unexpected in Chesa's space, which did not surprise Max. They walked back into the corridor, their eyes adjusting after the brighter bedrooms. This time Max stopped at the armoire and leaned against it.

Where else can I look? he wondered. Sty was certain that Josephine kept everything she acquired close at hand. Surely Josephine was responsible for more of the pieces on his uncle's list, and if so, they were in this apartment. Chesa opened her mouth to speak just as Max held up a hand.

"Wait." He spun to face the armoire. "What is this doing here?"

"It is for extra clothing, or what is not—"

Max was not listening to Chesa. He drew a flashlight from his pocket and snapped it on. "This is junk," he said, sweeping the cupboard with a narrow beam. He tried the handle. Locked.

"My bag," he said to Chesa.

She slipped it off her shoulder, having brought it along when they left Miss Wainwright's study. Chesa thought this dashing young spy might want the bag.

Max extracted a small pry bar and wedged one end between the armoire's two doors. It gave with some exertion. Max pulled both doors open, and the two of them were staring at empty space.

The back of the armoire had wide wooden slats. Max did not spend time searching for a catch, but slipped the teeth of the pry bar into a crack. Then he pushed the other end. One slat gave way, splintering where the metal forced it. Max used the lever to make room for slipping a hand behind the slat. When he pulled at the wood, a large piece broke off.

Shining his light through the hole, Max discovered a cavity lined with shelves. On each shelf sat objects Bedford Stuyvesant had catalogued. His nephew grinned as he stripped away the remaining boards. Max liked finding things.

Chesa had gone for the cart and empty boxes. She returned to find her new friend the spy inside the hiding place.

"Here," he said, handing out a delicately painted vase. "This, too."

As each piece came out through the armoire's broken back, Chesa cradled it carefully and then set it on the cart.

"That's it," Max said, stepping out of the hidden closet. "Let's get this stuff wrapped and boxed."

Both bent to the work of swaddling art, and in half an hour, they had wrapped several million dollars' worth of goods. They were silent, working swiftly, until the doorbell stopped them both.

Max's head snapped up. "Are you expecting someone?"

Chesa trembled, wishing she was not so scared in front of this boy. The doorbell rang again.

"What should I do?" Chesa asked.

The phone at Max's hip buzzed. He ignored it, but the buzzing continued. The doorbell, meanwhile, was silent. Max pulled up his phone and read the screen: *Let me in*.

"Chesa," Max said. "Go answer the door."

She scowled; her eyebrows met. Was he sure, this brazen American? Would this be the end of her young, promising life? She scuttled toward the entrance, wishing there was more to mourn. Chesa twisted the deadbolt, took the knob, and turned.

28

The door flew open.

Max had stayed several steps behind Chesa, ready to assist. When the door burst open, his jaw dropped.

"Galena?"

The young woman from the plane stood before him, her eyes flashing their slightly different colors.

"We can talk later. Right now, the clock is ticking. I left Josephine at the café with Renard; told her I needed a few minutes to make sure our shop was ready for her visit."

"You're the caterer?" Max sputtered.

She nodded. "I'm also the expediter. Bedford gave me this gig, since I knew my way around Portugal and a kitchen. How're you doing here?"

Max blinked, trying to recalibrate. More to discuss with his uncle once he got back home. "Everything's packed. I guess you're supposed to put it on the freight elevator?"

"Yep," she said. "But there's one other problem."

Figures, Max thought. "What's that?"

"Renard thinks she's gonna blow this joint, and although the man is a reptile, I'm inclined to believe him. Same with your uncle Sty," she said, staring at Max. "I checked."

"Great," said Max. "So you're telling me there's a bomb in here and we need to get out?"

"It's worse than that. I'm saying that if she discovers she's been set up, she'll level the place for sure. This woman is not playing with a full deck."

"Miss Wainwright hates games," Chesa said.

Galena ignored her.

"But how will she know—?" Max began.

Galena looked at him. "Two reasons. One, when she goes to the address I gave her, she's going to find a bakery that's closed for a family vacation. Two, Renard might just tip her off out of spite, since he hasn't been able to get what he wants."

"Renard? I thought he was on our side."

"He's on his own side. That, and he's probably ticked about not making off with Bedford's book." She nodded at the sheaf of paper Max held. "Having the place blow might be his way of sending a message."

"So let's—. Wait. That was you, last night? That happened?" Max asked.

This time, Galena ignored him. "We don't have a lot of time here," she said.

Max caught up. "Chesa and I put all her stuff in boxes. We can just run before she hits the switch."

Galena's head was shaking. "Your uncle ever tell you about the time she blew a place in Rio?"

"No."

"She took out a city block."

"Oh."

"This condo is full of people, to say nothing about the buildings around it, since it's summer. So," she said, looking at Max sternly. "Are you in? Bedford says you're good at this. Is he right?"

226

Max didn't stay for a reply but spun toward Josephine's study. From what he remembered of his uncle's briefing, this woman refused to let anyone else have what she could not keep or give away. The bomb would be in her special room.

He'd already searched for a compartment large enough to hide the items they'd found behind the armoire. Explosives would need less space, but still: where would they be?

With deft strokes of his knife, Max shredded the leather sofa and an armchair. He rifled every drawer in the desk and pulled more books off shelves.

The clock was running.

Where next? Max looked up, to see Chesa in the doorway. Galena stood behind her.

"Get out of here," Max said. "Go."

"Where?" Galena asked.

Max shut the knife, clicked it open, shut it, trying to think. "Do you have any ideas?" he asked Chesa.

The Filipina shook her head, and then stopped. "Baskerville," she said.

"Baskerville?"

"The dog. Usually he sleeps there in his ugly bed." She pointed at the jumble of blankets in the low, broad wicker basket. "It's strange," she said, quietly.

"What is?" Max asked.

"Miss Wainwright does not usually take Baskerville outside herself. She has me do that."

Looking past Chesa, Max spoke to Galena. "She knows."

"Or suspects," Galena answered.

Max stared at the dog's bed again. So big, and so ugly for this room. Ugly, he thought, like the armoire.

He jumped toward the wicker basket and bent to pat the blankets there. The lumps weren't soft, but hard, angular. Max carefully lifted the dingy fabric.

Beneath layers of plaid flannel, grey blocks had been carefully arranged around the perimeter of the basket. A series of wires ran from each brick of C-4 to a detonator that was connected to a radio device.

"Found it," Max said over his shoulder.

Galena was close now, with Chesa behind her.

"Can you kill this bomb?" the triathlete asked.

Max nodded. "I don't think Josephine really planned on someone being in here when she sent a signal." He pointed at Chesa. "My bag."

The girl scooped it from the cart and hurled it at Max. He pulled pliers from a side pocket. Then Max reached into the nest of cabling below him.

He pinched a zebra wire, snipping through the white and black plastic wrapping with the pliers. The receiver's green light turned red.

Using the pliers to nose through more of the tangle, Max found another wire and snipped again. The red light blinked out.

He stood, facing Galena. "Does your expediting extend to knowing a cop in this neighborhood?"

"Yeah." She drew a cell phone from her pocket and keyed in numbers. When a person answered, Galena rattled off a rapid string of instructions, in Portuguese. She finished, closed the phone and raised an eyebrow at Max's stare.

"What?" she said. "My dad was posted in Brazil, OK? I went to school there, so no big deal. You ready? Let's get out of here."

29

Satisfied that the tattooed woman Renard had introduced possessed the skills necessary for catering her
party, Josephine had agreed on a visit to her shop.
Yes, of course, she would come along shortly; it was
perfectly reasonable to allow a few moments to arrange platters for viewing. After the young woman
excused herself from the table, Josephine watched her
go, wondering why she had not anticipated the interest
of a client for this very purpose. Should a caterer not
be prepared for any eventuality?

Josephine turned her face to the sun. A few
minutes each day in the fresh air was important, but
not so much as to damage one's skin. She adjusted the
wide hat, reached for the last sip of coffee. Renard,
staring at faint traces of foam on the sides of his glass,
was silent in the chair across the table from her. Josephine set her demitasse on its saucer and instructed her
Frenchman to hail a cab so that she might locate the
caterer's shop in order to sample her wares.

The tattoos were troublesome; they would have to
be covered during the party. Had time not been against
her, Josephine would have looked elsewhere, but she
decided to trust the references Renard had provided.
She was, however, unlikely to recommend this sort of

person to others for any future business, given such patently poor taste.

Monsieur Renard drained the last of his beer. Then he rose and signaled a taxi idling further down the block. He returned to the table and made his apologies: other pressing engagements would keep him from accompanying Josephine to the caterer's shop. This she could understand; the man was so utterly resourceful that his services must be in great demand. She bade him farewell, after thanking him for such timely assistance.

When Josephine arrived at the address the tattooed hussy had supplied, she had a moment of confusion. A sign hanging in the door of the establishment indicated that the place was closed, a fact confirmed by shutters on the windows. Curiously, a man sat at a table beneath a striped umbrella directly outside the bakery, reading a newspaper.

She smelled trouble, and began to calculate her next moves: walk briskly to the bank's outside teller for as much cash as she could withdraw; continue on to the station with her beloved Baskerville and buy a ticket on the next train departing Faro; blow up the apartment using her cell phone.

Josephine turned to leave, but something about this man piqued her curiosity. She paused to inspect him from a distance. An American, judging by his clothes and the casual slouch of his demeanor. Older, too, about her age. She looked more closely. The beard was new.

As she approached the table, he stood and then pulled out a second chair.

"I understand congratulations are in order," the man said. He pulled a bottle from an ice bucket next to his own chair and filled two flutes with champagne. "On the occasion of your birthday."

The ride back to London didn't include Renard after all; the French Englishman never showed up for the flight.

At Heathrow, Max returned to the airline lounge. There, he folded a sheet of stationery around a stack of crisp Franklins and an airline ticket to Los Angeles, and tucked everything into an envelope with a Dutch address. Max hoped he'd spelled the name of Pieter de Groot's university correctly. After providing Max with stamps, the concierge promised to mail the packet that very day.

Max did not bother, again, with trying to find a way downtown during his layover. Instead he enjoyed a hot shower in the airline lounge, followed by fresh croissants and coffee.

Once home, he called Fire about meeting to talk over coffee. Max wanted to help his friend find a ring.

Thanks

Back when phones had cords (and came in maybe three colors), my family left suburban America to spend a year in West Africa. On our way, we stopped in Lisbon, and I recall one magical evening at an outdoor café where we ate a late supper and watched a trained monkey do tricks. Ever since, I've wanted to go back to Portugal.

More recently, a friend asked if I'd be writing a novel during National Novel Writing Month. I thought this was a particularly loopy idea, but tried to respond politely. The next year, however, towards the middle of October, my mind changed completely. Thanks to Sara Pike for the nudge.

This novel was written—mostly—in a month, but after that, there was plenty more to do. A fair bit of uncertainty, too, as with it, I got even further from 'serious' writing. But then more friends reminded me that when it comes to eating, dessert is not a bad thing.

I stepped over the edge when a call for beta readers yielded enthusiastic replies. And so, my gratitude to Lisa Befus, Kris Kailey, Cyndi Canner, Elaine Gegel, Dave Robinson, Martha Anderson, Tom Rennard, Anne Marie Kirkland, Kim Mouw, Tara Schneider, Rich Hannibal, Lynne Cosby, and Gina Solano for reading, commenting and pushing back.

Thanks to Chuck Bergstrom and Paul Schmidt for some needed technical advice, too.

As with *Playa Perdida*, Cherie Fieser applied her editor's skill to the manuscript. I appreciate her sharp eye, and that she uses a pencil instead of a red pen. Also as before, I made a few changes after Cherie finished—so what errors as may yet linger, *mea culpa*.

Writing puts me in a good mood but also limits human contact (and no, those aren't related). My family has figured this out. Their email, texts, and occasional visits keep me connected; they also understand my glazed looks and the itch to get back to the keyboard. Once again, I couldn't imagine attempting this sort of thing without them. Not only that, but part way through this project, we added one to the gang— another artist who knows something about these ropes. Thanks, Josh, for planning a wedding that meant a few days away from the basement study.

Lastly, *merci* to Della Royal, my middle school French teacher, who required her students not only to attempt speaking the language but to write stories in it. I remember handing in one about spies and thieves that was, being in French, somewhat underdeveloped. But thanks to Miss Royal, I figured out how much I like chases, and motley crews.

Also by Dan Schmidt

Unexpected Wisdom:
Major Wisdom from the Minor Prophets

Taken by Communion:
How the Lord's Supper Nourishes the Soul

Playa Perdida

Our Savior Come:
An Advent Companion

—*AVAILABLE AT ONLINE RETAILERS*—

For more information—
WWW.TOUCANIC.NET